BLACK BEAUTY

Retold by Rod Huron
Color Illustrations by Helle Urban

Contents

CHAPTER 1

My Home

Mother's name was "Duchess," but our master called her "Pet." He liked her more than he did his other horses.

And I think he liked me better than the other colts, even though I was the littlest.

We lived in a pretty place. There were six of us colts. We had a big field to run in, and a little stream down at the low end, and a pond.

There were trees for shade, and water lilies on the pond. I liked my home.

I didn't always like the other colts, though. Sometimes they kicked and bit. They could be rough.

One time when they were getting rowdy, Mother whinnied to me and called me over to where she was.

"I need to tell you something," she said. "You're a special colt. You know how famous your father is. Your grandfather was famous, too. He won the cup at Newmarket two times."

She looked at me. "Have you ever seen me kick or bite?"

"No," I told her. I knew Mother was trying to teach me something, and I could tell it was important.

Then she went on. "Your grandmother was as gentle a horse as there ever was. I've tried to be that way, too. And I want you to grow up to be gentle and good. I hope you'll not become unruly and mean like some horses can be."

I've tried to remember what Mother said.

It wasn't hard to be gentle, living where we did. Our master treated us as if we were his own family. He saw to it that our food was good, and that we always had enough, and that our stable was good, too.

Sometimes he even brought me a piece of bread, or a carrot for Mother.

He liked Mother. When he went to town, he usually had Mother pull his buggy for him, and she liked doing that.

Our master was a busy man, so he had Daniel to look after us horses. Old Daniel was as good as the master was.

Yes, I liked my home.

But not everybody was nice. There was a boy named Dick, a plowboy from one of the farms, and he would come into our field to pick some of the blackberries that grew along the fence.

We didn't mind that, but when he ate all the berries he wanted, he thought it was fun to throw rocks or sticks at us colts and make us run. We could always gallop down to the other end of the field, but those rocks hurt.

5

I didn't like it when Dick came around. One day he was tormenting us, and he didn't know our master was right there in the next field.

Our master gave Dick a surprise. When he saw Dick throwing sticks at us, the master was over the fence in an instant and he let Dick have it.

"You're fired! You're finished. I thought I told you to never do this again. You're a bad boy. Leave this farm and don't come back."

That was the last we ever saw of Dick.

Could I tell you something which happened when I was not quite two years old? That was a long time ago, but I still remember.

It was early in the spring, and the other colts and I were down at the low end of the field. The grass was really good there.

Away off in the distance we heard dogs coming.

One of the other colts was older and knew what it was. Raising his head, he listened.

"Those are the hounds," he explained. Then he turned and went down to the end of the field, and the rest of us went along with him.

Mother was already there, and one of our master's old riding horses was, too. They seemed to know what was happening. Then, as I looked across over the hedge, I could see dogs running across the next field.

How can I tell you what the noise was like? It wasn't barking. It wasn't a howl or a whine. It was more like a "Yo! yo, ooh. Yo! yo, oh, ooh!"

Then I saw men, a lot of them, everybody in green coats, coming behind the dogs, riding fast. They were riding across the field as fast as if it were a smooth road.

I wanted to go, too. All of us colts did. Everybody but Mother. Even the master's old riding horse snorted and stamped around.

But the noise passed by us as the riders and their horses went way down into another field. Then the noise stopped.

I stretched my head as far as I could and tried to see. The dogs had quit barking, and and were going here and there, sniffing the ground. The horses waited while the men, still on the horses, watched.

The old horse explained things to us. "The dogs have lost the scent." Then he added, "Maybe the hare will get away."

"What hare?" I wanted to know.

"They are chasing a hare; a rabbit," he told me. "It could be one that lives in our hedge; it could be one from another farm. It doesn't matter to them what hare it is, just so they can run after it."

One of the dogs started to yowl again, and the others joined in. Dogs and horses and men started coming back toward us.

"We may get a look at the hare," my mother said.

Then I saw it, terror in its eyes, trying to get away.

9

The dogs were right behind and chased it down toward the brook. Didn't they know about the steep bank?

The dogs jumped over the bank and splashed through the stream and went tearing across the field.

Then the huntsmen came. Six or eight horses made it over the stream, nearly trampling the dogs.

Now the hare was at the fence and tried to get through, but couldn't, and when she turned and made for the road the dogs were on her. I didn't know hares could make a sound, but this one did.

Onc of the huntsmen rode up and kicked the dogs out of the way and held up what was left of the hare, all torn and bleeding. I couldn't understand why everyone seemed so pleased.

When I turned away I saw what was going on by the brook, and I almost turned away again. Two horses lay on the ground; one in the stream, trying to get up; the other on the grass, making awful sounds.

One of the riders was coming out of the water all covered with mud. The other rider lay still and didn't move.

"He's hurt badly. His neck may be broken," said my mother.

"Serves him right," one of the colts said, but Mother stopped him.

"No," she said. "Don't talk like that. I don't understand why they like to hunt, and sometimes hurt their horses and hurt themselves. But they like the sport and we are only horses and don't understand."

While we watched, we could see the men trying to help the boy who was hurt. They tried to lift him, but his head fell back and his arm hung down. No one made noise now; even the dogs were quiet.

Finally the men picked him up and carried him across the field to our master's house. I heard later that it was young George Gordon. His family's only son, too.

But that wasn't the end of it. One of the riders went off to bring Mr. Bond, the farrier who takes care of horses, and he came and looked at the black horse still lying on the grass, trying to get up.

Someone ran off to the master's house and brought back a gun. There was a loud bang and an awful shriek from the horse and then it was still.

CHAPTER 2

Learning to Work

O f course, every horse has to earn his keep, so I couldn't stay in my meadow forever. When I was four years old and full grown, my master was ready to sell me. What kind of owner would the new person be?

Do you remember the boy who died in the hunt I told you about? His father, Squire Gordon, was one of the people who came to look at me.

My coat was jet black, except for one white foot and a white blaze on my forehead. People said I was handsome.

Squire Gordon looked into my eyes and my mouth. He felt my legs and my sides and my back. I had to walk, and then trot, then gallop, and walk again, while he watched.

He seemed to like me. "He needs to be broken in," the Squire said, "and then I'll buy him."

Do you know what "breaking in" means? Let me tell you.

It means teaching a horse to wear a saddle and bridle, to carry a man or woman or child on his back, and to go this way and that, fast or slow, as the rider wishes.

It means teaching the horse to wear the straps and cords which let him pull a wagon or carry a person. It means having a collar around his neck and a crupper under his tail.

It means wearing breeching straps and the nose piece and the rest of the harness.

At first I didn't like it, but in time I learned to stand still while someone put the harness on me, and to go forward, or turn left, or turn

16

right, or stand still—whatever command the driver gave me.

This wasn't as bad as it sounds. I didn't want to stay in the stable all day, and wearing a harness made it possible for me to pull a buggy or a light gig and be outside and enjoy seeing the sights. I liked that.

I learned not to jump or jerk whenever I saw or heard something unusual. I learned not to speak to other horses. I learned to do whatever the driver wanted me to do, even if I was tired or hungry.

I didn't learn all of this at once, but I'm telling you this so you can see how important it is for a horse to be "broken in."

Breaking in was so important my master wanted to do it himself.

I could tell by the way my master spoke to me again and again, so gentle yet so firm, that he was preparing me for something special.

After I had my oats, he kept coaxing me, and while he kept talking to me he put a metal bit into my mouth and then fixed the bridle to the piece of metal.

I didn't like that at all. Would you like to have a cold, hard, rod of steel in your mouth? The bit went over my tongue, and the ends stuck out the sides of my mouth. Straps were fastened to the bit and these straps went around my chin and over my head and under my throat.

I didn't like wearing the bit, but I wore it anyway. There was no way I could get out of it.

Several days after I had learned to wear the bit, it was time for the saddle.

At first, I didn't like the saddle, either. But Old Daniel took his time and was gentle as he talked to me and put the straps on me and then eased the saddle on my back.

He gave me some oats, too, and I liked that. In a few minutes he took the saddle off.

Every day after that for a while, he came and gave me oats and put the saddle on.

Before long I started looking forward to wearing the saddle, and getting the oats.

One morning after Old Daniel had put on my saddle, the master got on. That was a surprise, but he wasn't heavy, and I easily carried him down through the field.

As master guided me, I caught on instantly. He was so careful with the reins that I could easily tell where he wanted to go.

For the next few days the master came every day and took me out. I liked that.

Next, I had to learn to wear shoes. I didn't like that. Master himself took me to the place where they would put on the shoes, so that I wouldn't be afraid.

The blacksmith came at me with a big knife, but it was okay. He picked up each foot and used the knife to trim away some of the hoof. I thought it would hurt, but it didn't.

Do you know what he did then? He took curved pieces of iron and nailed them to my feet! It didn't hurt, but these things made my feet feel stiff and heavy.

I became accustomed to them, but it took awhile.

After all that, we still weren't done. The next thing was the harness. First, they put an awkward thing on my neck—that was the collar—and a bridle. The bridle had leather pieces next to my eyes so that I could only see straight ahead. These made me nervous. But that wasn't the worst.

The worst was when they put a little saddle on my back with a strap which went under my tail. That thing was the crupper. I hated it. I didn't like having my long tail doubled up and poked through that strap. It was almost as bad as the bit in my mouth.

If I ever felt like kicking, it was then; but I didn't want to hurt my master.

Master knew I needed to learn something else, so he sent me for a couple of weeks to a neighboring farmer who had a field next to a railroad.

The first train! It scared me! I was feeding, minding my own business—there were cows in the field but I didn't bother them—when I heard this strange sound in the distance and it kept coming closer.

The noise! Suddenly there was a long, black machine belching smoke. I ran to the other side of the field, and would have gone farther if it had not been for the fence.

I had hardly calmed down from that one when another one came by: the same horrible noise and smoke. It scared me again.

But the trains always stayed out of the field, and once in a while one of them slowed down and stopped at the station close by.

They made an even worse noise as they were stopping, but they never came into the field, and the cows didn't seem to be concerned. I learned that I didn't have to be afraid, and I wasn't.

I'm glad my master knew I needed to learn about trains, because later on I saw many horses which were afraid of steam engines. I was glad that I wasn't afraid.

One of the best parts of my breaking in was when my master put me and my mother in double harness and let us work together.

Mother was a good teacher, and when my breaking in was finished, I was ready for whatever work my new master wanted me to do. I moved to Squire Gordon's place in early May.

CHAPTER 3

Squire Gordon's Estate

Squire Gordon's estate was called Birt-wick Park, and was at the village called Birtwick. In fact, the estate was bigger than the village. Squire Gordon was a rich man.

When it was time to leave, my master came and said good-bye. "Be a good horse," he told me, "and always do your best."

I couldn't say good-bye, so I put my nose into his hand and he patted me and I left the place where I grew up.

Maybe I ought to tell you what Birtwick Park was like, since I lived there for several years.

At the entrance was a big iron gate, and there was a lodge just inside the gate. Then you went along a tree-lined road until you came to a second lodge and another gate, and then you were at the house and the gardens.

Beyond this was the paddock and stables, and the orchard. Squire Gordon had many horses and carriages, but I'll just tell about the stable where I lived. It was nice, with lots of room and a door window that opened onto the yard.

My first stall was what is called a loose box. That means I wasn't tied up; I could walk around or lie down if I wanted to. It's great to have a loose box.

The groom put me here and brought me some oats and corn. I thought this must be a good place.

There was a little pony in the stall next to me, and I asked him what his name was.

He had a halter on, so he couldn't turn all the way around.

"Merrylegs," he told me. "I carry the Squire's daughters on my back, and sometimes take my mistress out in the low chair."

Then Merrylegs asked me, "Are you going to live next to me?"

"Yes," I said.

"Then," said Merrylegs, "I hope you don't bite. I don't want someone next door who has a bad temper."

Just then a horse in the stall on the other side of Merrylegs looked over at us. It was a beautiful chestnut color, but its ears were laid back, and its eyes were angry.

"So you're the one who turned me out of my box," she said. "How is it that a youngster like you puts a lady out of her home?"

"I'm sorry," I said. "It wasn't anything I did. Here's where they put me. Maybe I'm not as old as you, but in all my four years I've never had any trouble with any other horse and I don't want trouble now."

27

When they took the chestnut colored horse out that afternoon, Merrylegs told me about her.

"They call her Ginger, because she snaps and bites," Merrylegs began. "She bit James, the stableboy, and made his arm bleed, so Miss Flora and Miss Jessie were afraid to come into the stable.

"The girls used to bring me an apple or a carrot, or maybe a piece of bread, but when Ginger stood in that box where you are, they were afraid to come near. You aren't like that, are you?"

I told him that I never bit anything but my food and that I didn't intend to start biting horses or people now.

"What pleasure does Ginger find in biting people, anyway?" I asked Merrylegs.

"I don't think she finds pleasure in it," he replied. "It's just a bad habit. Maybe someone was mean to her once. But the people here aren't mean. John is the best groom in every

way, and you never saw such a good boy as James. It's Ginger's own fault she was turned out of that box."

Next morning John Manly, the coachman, took me into the yard and brushed my coat until it was soft and clean. Squire Gordon came to look at me, and he seemed pleased.

"John," he said, "would you take the new horse around after breakfast and see how he does?"

So after breakfast, John came and fitted me with a bridle and saddle. He was gentle and careful to fit everything just right.

He rode slowly at first, then at a trot, then a canter. When we were out in the open land we went into a gallop.

"Ho, ho! my boy," he said as he pulled me to a stop. "I think you would like to follow the hounds."

On our way back to the stable, we met Squire and Mrs. Gordon. They came over to where we were and John jumped off.

"Well, John, what do you think?"

"He's grand, sir," answered John. "He is fast, and with a good spirit, and a light rein is all it takes to guide him. He isn't afraid at all. Even the noise in the town didn't bother him. Yes, sir; he's a good horse."

The next day the master wanted to ride me. I tried to remember what my mother had told me about being gentle and doing what my master wanted.

The Squire was a good rider, and made it easy for me. His lady met us when we rode up.

"How do you like him, dear?" she asked.

"He is as good a horse as I've ever seen," the Squire replied. "We ought to give him a name. What should we call him?"

"We could call him Ebony, since he is so black. Or how about Blackbird, after your uncle's horse?"

"No," Squire Gordon told his wife, "this is a better looking horse than old Blackbird."

31

Looking at my face and my coat, she suggested, "Let's call him Black Beauty."

I liked my new name. Black Beauty. And I liked Squire Gordon. I was content with my new life. The only thing I could have wished for was my liberty. To be able to run when I wanted; to lie down when I wanted; to toss my tail and gallop rather than have to stand still and wait.

But that was not to be. I had work to do.

Before long, Ginger and I began to pull the carriage together. At first I was afraid she would nip at me, or not pull her share of the load, but my fears were unfounded.

Now and then we had time to talk. When Ginger learned about my growing up years and my breaking in, it made her sad.

"If I had the kind of home you had," she told me, "then I would have had a better chance than I did. Maybe I wouldn't have such trouble with my temper. The way it is now, I don't know if I can ever change."

"Why not?" I asked her.

"Because things have been hard for me," she began. "Until I came here, no man or beast was ever kind to me.

"The man who broke me in was especially mean. I was in the field, and before I knew it, several men came after me, and cornered me, and grabbed my nose. They held me and jammed the bit in my mouth and forced the halter on my head and started to drag me

33

along while one of them went behind with a whip and kept hitting me.

"It was terrible. I fought, but it was no use. Even the old master, Mr. Ryder, didn't seem to care. He was not mean like the others, but his son, Samson, was strong and very rough.

"Yes, it was hard for me. I was sold to a man in London to make a pair with another chestnut horse. He liked our color, and wanted his horses to be stylish. Ohh, when he put on the 'bearing rein.'"

Ginger groaned when she remembered.

"What is a bearing rein?" I asked.

"A cruel and horrible device," she said emphatically. "They pull your head back and fasten the bearing rein to the saddle. You can't have your head free and your neck hurts and it's hard to walk and worse to pull.

"They even put a second bit in your mouth. It's awful for a minute, much less for hours."

Ginger stamped her foot, then she went on. "I know that's why I am short tempered. When you're mistreated, and no one takes any care for you, it's hard to keep from becoming mean and ill-tempered yourself."

"At least John and James are kind to us here," I suggested.

"Yes," Ginger agreed. "I'm glad for that. I hope I never have to leave."

Our master liked to ride Ginger, with the mistress on me, and the girls on Merrylegs and another horse named Sir Oliver. All of us—people and horses—enjoyed our rides together.

I had it best of all, because I always carried the mistress. She was so light, and her hand was light on the rein, too. I barely felt her guiding me.

A horse's mouth is tender, and we can be guided without jerking or hard pulls. I think that's why the mistress always preferred me. Ginger's mouth was spoiled by the way she

35

was broken in, and by the gag bit she had worn in London.

Sir Oliver had a short tail, only six or seven inches long.

"Did you have an accident?" I wanted to know.

"Accident!" he snorted. "Sheer butchery, I'd say. When I was young, my master had someone cut my tail in two; right through the flesh and the bone." He snorted again, remembering.

"How awful!"

"Yes," he agreed. "The pain was terrible. And it hurt for a long time. But the thing I most regret is the loss of my long, beautiful tail. Not only do I look unsightly, but now I have nothing to use to keep the flies away from my sides and my legs. When they dig into me and bite and sting it nearly drives me crazy."

"Why did your master do this to you?" asked Ginger.

"Because they think it looks good," Sir Oliver answered.

"That must be the reason they use the bearing rein," said Ginger.

"It is indeed," said Sir Oliver. "Because they think it looks good! They wouldn't do such things to their own children, would they? Why do they do it to us?"

CHAPTER 4

Danger in the Night

One December day after John brought me back from my morning exercise, the master came into the stable. He looked like he had something on his mind. James was in the grain room getting some oats.

"Good morning, John," said the master.

"Good morning, sir."

The master had a question: "Have you any complaints to make of James?"

"Complaints? No, sir."

"Is he a good worker? Is he respectful?"

"Yes, sir," answered John. "Always. He does his work and does it well, whether or not I'm there watching."

"What about when he takes the horses out or runs an errand?" continued the master. "Does he waste his time? Does he stop at places he shouldn't?"

"No, sir," John answered. "Is someone saying that James is dishonest or that he's bad? You can trust James, sir. He's steady. He's cheerful. In fact, he's as smart a young fellow as I've ever had in this stable."

John paused to give the master a chance to speak, but the master just stood there.

So John went on.

"Sir, if someone is saying bad things about James, they are wrong. James is as good a man as you can find. He's good with the horses. He knows them and he's gentle with them and always considers his horse. Yes, sir, James would never hurt a horse, he wouldn't."

All this time the master said nothing, but now he relaxed and looked pleased.

Unknown to John, James had come in from the grain room and had been standing behind

40

him and had heard some of what John was saying about him.

"Come here, James," the master told him. John, surprised, turned around, then looked back at the master.

"Nothing to be worried about," the master told them both. "James, I'm glad our friend John here has such a good opinion of you and of your work. And I may say that his opinion supports my own. You see, my brother-in-law, Sir Clifford Williams, of Clifford Hall, is in need of a trustworthy young groom. His old coachman has been with him twenty years and is getting on, so Cliff wants to find a younger man to work with the old man and be ready to step into his place. That's the reason for the questions."

So James was to depart for Clifford Hall. Although I was sorry to hear that he was leaving us, the next few weeks were good ones for me. John wanted James to be fully trained, so he had James take me out every day for practice in driving.

41

I never knew the carriage to go out so often before. Sometimes the mistress went out; sometimes the master; sometimes the young ladies; and sometimes it was only for an errand.

I learned a lot during these few weeks. James took me to all kinds of places. I learned to make my way through city traffic, as well as how to get around the railway station, the bridges, the narrow streets, and the wide ones, too.

Yes, I was sorry to see James Howard go, but these last few weeks of his training were good experience for me.

Before James left, my master and mistress decided to visit some friends who lived two days' journey from Birtwick Park.

The first day we had to go up and down some long hills, but James was so careful that Ginger and I didn't mind the climb at all. He always made for the smoothest part of the road, and now and then would set the carriage crossways to the road so we could rest a bit.

On the way down the other side James kept the drag-brake on, to make it easier for us. He always remembered to take it off at the right place, too.

Some drivers are so thoughtless as to leave the drag on even when going uphill. You can imagine what that does to the horses.

Just as the sun went down, we reached the town where the master planned to stay the night. The hotel was in the Market Place, and we drove under an archway into a long yard which had the stables and coach-houses at the far end.

The chief groom was an active little man who wore a yellow striped waistcoat. He had a bad limp but it didn't keep him from working.

Before I knew it he had my harness un-buckled. With a pat and a good word, he led me down to the stable. Another man did the same with Ginger. James stood by while the men rubbed us down and cleaned our feet and shoes.

This old groom was as gentle as he was quick. When he was finished, James seemed unable to believe someone could do such a good job so easily.

"Well, sir," James told the old man, "you beat anything I ever saw."

"Practice makes perfect," said the old man. "T'would be a pity if forty years didn't make a difference. Yessir; forty years I've been doin' this.

"I was a jockey til I had a fall and broke my leg, so no more ridin' for me. But I couldn't live without being around horses, so I took to workin' for hotels. I'm still at it."

The little man straightened up, trying to get the kinks out of his back. "You've a good horse here. I can tell when they've been cared for. Yessir, give me twenty minutes with a horse and I know what sort of groom he's had."

He looked me over, then said to James, "Now see this one. He's gentle. He doesn't fidget. He lets you clean his feet. He's not afraid of people. He's a good one, he is."

45

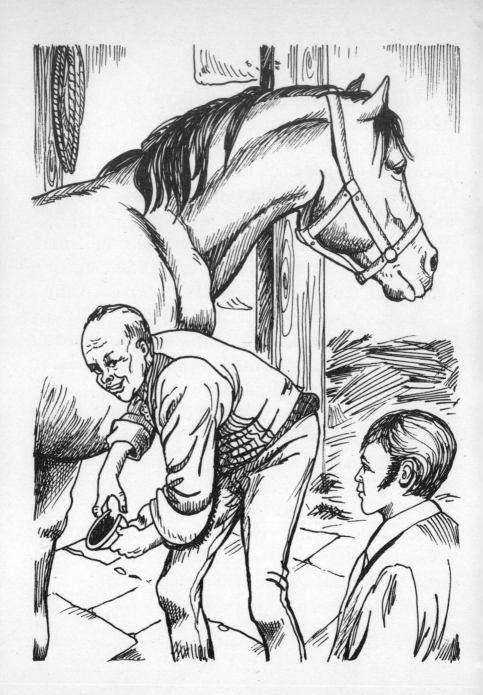

Finished, the little man took off his coat
and prepared to leave.

"You should see some of the poor crea-
tures which come in here," he said to James.
"They're a bundle of nerves. Bad tempered.
Won't stand still or let you work with them.
Some horses have it hard, they do."

When the groom had finished, James and
the others left us.

Later on that same evening, the groom
brought in another horse which had been on
the road all day. While the groom worked
with the horse, there was a young man standing there, watching, smoking a pipe while he
and the groom talked.

"I say, Towler," said the groom, "put out that
pipe and throw down some hay for me."

"Sure," the young man answered, and disappeared up the trap door. I could hear him
walking overhead, and the sounds of him
putting down the hay.

James came in for one more look at Ginger and me and then the men left and we were alone for the night.

I don't know how long I slept, and I'm not sure what time I woke up—but it was pitch black and I couldn't breathe.

The air was thick and choking. I heard Ginger coughing, and the other horses snorting and moving about.

Smoke. The stable was full of smoke. It seemed to be coming through the trap door to the hayloft.

Then I heard it—a soft, rushing noise; a low crackling and snapping. Fire! The stable was on fire!

I could hear the other horses pulling at their halters and stamping and bumping against the sides of their stalls, but the smoke was so thick I couldn't see them. All of us sensed the danger.

The smoke kept getting worse.

I heard someone running and yelling.

48

Suddenly the door burst open. It was the old groom with a lantern. Working quickly he untied the first horse and led her outside, then came back for the second.

Worse. The smoke was worse. Through the trap door to the loft I could see flickers of orange and yellow and red.

Another man came in and tried to untie a horse, but he was frantic and made the horse nervous — it was already scared — so the horse wouldn't move. The man tried to save several horses, pulling and dragging, but none of them would go with him. Finally he disappeared through the doorway.

With the outside air coming in, breathing was better, but it made the fire worse. Now there was a whooshing sound, and through the trap door I could see that the fire was brighter, growing stronger and making a roaring sound.

It was terrible.

Then I heard James' voice, calm as ever.

"Come, come, it's time for us to leave. Wake up, now."

Since I was nearest the door, he came to me first.

"Come on, Beauty. Let's get your bridle on. We'll soon be out of here." He had a scarf around his neck and he took it off and covered my eyes with it. Patting me and coaxing, he led me outside.

As soon as I was safe, he went back for Ginger. When I saw him go, I gave out a shrill whinny. Ginger told me afterwards that my whinny was all that gave her the courage to come through the smoke.

The yard was in chaos. Horses being brought out. Carriages being pulled out of sheds. Men yelling and running.

But I watched only the stable door—where James had gone—to see if he would come back from the flames and smoke. To see if Ginger would escape.

Then I heard my master shouting: "James Howard! James! Where are you?"

Suddenly there was a crashing noise inside as something caved in, and everyone standing around me started and jumped back. The roof

was on fire now, and through the cracks in the building I could see flashes of red.

Then I saw James, coming through the smoke, leading Ginger. I gave out a joyful neigh, even though Ginger was coughing and tossing her head up and down.

"Good work," said master. "You're a brave lad. Are you hurt, son?"

James still couldn't say anything, he had breathed so much smoke. He nodded his head to show he was okay.

The master had me, and James had Ginger. We were making our way through the yard toward the entry when we heard the rumble of wheels and the sound of horses coming at a gallop.

People were shouting. "Make way for the fire engine! Out of the way!"

Clattering and thundering over the cobblestones, two huge horses dashed into the yard, the heavy engine behind them. The fire was coming through the roof now.

Master wanted to get away from there. He led me, and James led Ginger, and we went out into the Market Place. How quiet it seemed, though we could still hear the commotion from the fire—men yelling, and the awful cries of two poor horses still inside, choking and burning to death in their stalls.

James and master found another hotel where they put us for the night. The next morning we heard people talking about how the fire started.

Yes, you guessed it.

It was from Dick Towler's pipe. When he went to the loft for the hay, he laid his pipe down.

Now the stable was gone. Only the walls still stood. Two horses lay buried under the burnt remains.

CHAPTER 5

A New Groom
and Troubles

The morning after the fire we started out again, and by evening reached the home of master's friend. How wonderful to be in a clean stable and a nice stall. The coachman made us comfortable, and when he heard how James rescued Ginger and me from the fire, he spoke more kindly to James.

"Young man," the coachman said to James, "it's nearly impossible to get horses out of a stable when there is either fire or flood. For some reason, animals seem more afraid to leave the stable than they do to stay. Your horses must really trust you or they would not have followed you out."

When we got home, John was glad to have us back, especially when he heard about the fire.

As he and James were putting things away from the trip, James asked, "Have you heard who they've hired to replace me?"

"Sure," John answered. "Do you know little Joe Green? He works at the Lodge."

"Little Joe Green! He's just a boy!"

"He's almost fifteen," said John.

"But he's just a boy!"

"So he is. He's a hard worker, though. And he's good to horses. Little Joe's dad put in a good word for him, and master seems willing to give the boy a chance."

"But he's so young...."

John kept talking. "Well, I said I'd give him a chance, too. I said I'd try him for six weeks. If he doesn't work out, then we'll look for someone else."

"Six weeks!" said James. "No one can learn much in six weeks!"

John thought for a moment.

"Let me tell you how it happened to me," John began. "I don't think I've ever told you, but I've been an orphan since I was fifteen. My parents took the fever and died within ten days of each other. It was just my sister Nelly and me, and not one relative or friend to help.

"I'm not complaining, but we had it hard. Nelly worked for a widow woman, and I took a job as a stableboy. The coachman was good to me. Norman was his name.

"Anyway, old Norman gave me a chance. He showed me things, little by little, so that by the time he couldn't work any longer, I was able to take his place."

"I see what you mean," John admitted. "I guess I'm ready to give a boy a chance just like someone gave me a chance."

"I suppose you're right," James agreed.

"Yes," John said. "This world would be a better place if we'd all give each other a hand

57

now and then and stop trying to shove everyone else out of the way."

Little Joe turned out to be a good worker. It took some time, though.

James had to show him how to sweep the stable, how to bring in the straw and spread it, how to throw down the hay, how to clean the harness, how to wash the carriage.

Seeing this young lad busy from morning to night made me realize all over again how much work there is in taking care of a stable.

Merrylegs didn't like the new boy at first. But before long even Merrylegs agreed that Little Joe was going to work out well.

Sorry as we were to see James leave, all of us felt good about having Little Joe Green.

A few days after James left for his job, I had eaten the hay Joe had put out for me and was fast asleep on my straw when the stable bell jarred me awake.

"Ring-ring! Ring-rrring!"

John's door opened and I could hear him running up to the house. He was back again in a minute, carrying a lantern. Rushing into the stable, he opened the door to my stall.

"Beauty! Get up. Get up. We've got a job to do tonight."

In no time I was saddled and bridled and ready to go. We headed up to the house where master was waiting. He had an awful look on his face.

"Now, John," he said, "ride as fast as you can to Doctor White. Tell him the mistress is ill. Every minute counts, lad. Here is a note to Doctor White. When you've delivered the note, go to the Inn and give Beauty a rest. Come back as soon as you can."

"Yes, sir," John said, and we were gone.

The gardener was ready with the gate open, and we were on our way. Through the Park and the sleeping village we galloped on, and John did not slow or stop until we came to the toll-gate.

The gate keeper's house was dark. Even before I was stopped John had swung down and was pounding on the door, calling for the toll-keeper.

"Wake up," he called. "Emergency. Wake up."

It was only a minute before the man appeared, but it seemed like an hour.

"Here," John told the sleepy figure, handing him the money. "The Doctor will be coming back. Here's payment for him, too. Keep the gate open so there won't be any delay."

And off we went again.

The road leveled out, wide and straight. John leaned closer and talked to me, coaxing me on. I could tell by his voice that this was urgent.

No need for a whip on me, so for two miles I galloped as fast as I've ever gone. My old grandfather must have run like that when he won the race at Newmarket.

When we came to the bridge, John slowed me down a bit and patted my neck.

61

"Well done, Beauty; good boy," he told me. I think he would have let me go slower, but my spirit was up and I was ready to run again.

The air was cool and crisp and the moon was bright enough to light the road. It was a night for speed. We pounded through a little village, probably waking a family or two, then a stretch with woods on either side, then up a little hill and down.

After eight miles, we finally came to the town. My footsteps echoed off the buildings as we clattered through the empty streets.

The tower clock rang three as we drew up at Doctor White's door. John rang the bell then hammered on the door with both fists.

Someone threw open an upstairs window. Doctor White, in nightclothes, put his head out. "What is it, my boy?"

"Mrs. Gordon is bad sick, sir. The Squire wants you to come at once. She is so sick he thinks she will die if something isn't done. Here is the message he sent."

"Wait," the Doctor said. "I'll be right down."

Minutes later he came out, dressed and ready. But where was his horse?

"The problem is," he began, "my horse has been out all day and is worn out. My son has my other one. Do you think I could borrow your horse?"

John wasn't sure. "He's come full speed nearly all the way, and I was to give him a rest here." John thought for a minute. "But I think the Squire wouldn't mind if you took him, sir."

So off I went again. The ride back was not so pleasant. The Doctor weighed more than John, and was not nearly such a good rider.

When we reached the toll-gate, the Doctor gave me a minute to rest, and I needed it. Then we were off.

By the time we reached Birtwick Park, I was nearly gone. Little Joe was at the gate and master was at the door. The Doctor went at once into the house, and Little Joe took me to the stable.

I was hot, my coat was soaking wet, and my legs trembled. All I could do was stand and pant.

Joe drew a full pail of water and I drank it all. He rubbed my legs and my chest, and gave me some hay and grain. Then he went to bed.

Before long I was shaking I was so cold. My whole body hurt. I ached everywhere. If only John were here, but he had those eight miles to walk back.

Restless, I laid down, but there was no way to be comfortable. I heard a moan, and realized it was my own sound.

At last John came. He was worn out, but in a moment he was bending over me.

"Ahh, Beauty," he said in a weary voice. "Look at you. No wonder you have a chill. Where is your blanket?"

Then he saw the bucket. "Why? Why?," he said again, and kicked the bucket aside. "He probably gave you a full pail, too! Cold water, after a run like that!"

John ran to the house for some hot water and made me a warm gruel. I drank part of it and I think I went to sleep.

By now I was very ill. It felt as if my lungs were on fire. Every breath hurt.

Night and day John nursed me, even rising in the night to see if I needed anything. Master came, too, several times.

I do not know how long I was sick. Mr. Bond, the horse doctor, came every day. Ginger and Merrylegs had been moved to the far end of the stable, so that I could have quiet. The fever affected my hearing, and every sound gave me pain. I could count the footsteps whenever someone passed between the stable and the house.

One night Thomas Green, Little Joe's father, came to help John give me some medicine.

After they had poured it down my throat, the two men sat down on a bench in Merrylegs' stall to see if I could stomach the medicine. They had set the lantern so the light did not bother me, but I could hear their voices as they talked low.

"I wish," Mr. Green said to John, "that you could find it in yourself to say a word of encouragement to my Joe. He knows he's the cause of this. He would never have hurt Beauty. No sir. He was only doing what he thought was right."

John didn't say anything for a moment or two. "I'm sorry, Tom. I didn't mean to hurt Little Joe. But look at what has happened. Beauty is a fine horse, and he made such a good run and saved the mistress's life, the doctor says. Now he's near to dying himself, because of a boy's carelessness."

"I know," Joe's father agreed. "Maybe it was carelessness. But it was not meanness. It wasn't his intention. He's just a boy, and he didn't know."

"A boy who didn't know better," John repeated. "You weren't so happy when the girls left your hothouse door open and the frost killed your plants. Ignorance can do a great deal of harm."

Tom nodded. "Yes, you're right. But have you ever been young, John?"

"Yes, I have," John admitted. Then, "Tomorrow I'll say something to Joe. I'll be kind; I know he meant no wrong."

CHAPTER 6

Little Joe
Becomes a Man

Joe Green soon made up for his mistake with me. John began to trust him again, although he still did not let Joe take either Ginger or me out very often.

One morning John was out with one of the other horses when master wanted a note taken right away to a businessman about three miles from Birtwick.

Joe was the only person available, so master told Joe to saddle me and take the note.

"Be careful with Beauty, Joe. He's not quite himself yet, so be gentle with him."

Joe needed no reminder, so our trip was not difficult at all. Joe delivered the note, and on the way home, just past the brickyard, we came upon a cart loaded down with bricks, its wheels half buried in mud.

The carter was yelling and whipping his horses unmercifully. Joe pulled up to look at the pitiful sight. The two horses struggled against the load, but they could not move it at all. Both animals were drenched in sweat, straining their best to move the overloaded wagon.

"Hey, sir," said Joe. "Hold the whip! No horses could move that cart, stuck as it is."

The driver ignored Joe's remarks, and went on lashing with his whip.

"Mister," Joe tried again. "Stop! I'll help you lighten the cart. It's too heavy for them."

Now the driver turned to face Joe, the whip raised and ready in his hand. Joe caught the smell of alcohol. Not only was the man angry, he was drunk.

"Mind your business, boy." With that the driver turned and began yelling and beating his horses again.

Something had to be done. In an instant, Joe turned me in the direction of the head brickmaker's house. We rode quickly, probably faster than my master would have liked.

"Mr. Clay," Joe called out as he knocked on the door. "Is Mr. Clay here?"

The door opened and Mr. Clay himself answered. "What is it, young man?"

Joe's words came all in a rush. "Sir, there's a man down past your brickyard with a cart stuck in the mud. He's going to beat his horses to death if someone doesn't stop him. I said I would help him lighten the cart, but he wouldn't, so I came here. Do something, sir."

Mr. Clay's face darkened. "I'll do that, son. And may I ask if you will be willing to go before the magistrate and give evidence of what you saw if I need it?"

"Yes, sir."

"I'll take care of it," Mr. Clay said quickly, and was gone.

We headed toward home. When we arrived, John could see that Joe was angry about something.

"What's wrong?" John wanted to know. When Joe told John what had happened, John was angry, too. "You did the right thing, my boy," he told Little Joe. "Many people wouldn't have bothered, but you did right. Yes, indeed."

By now Joe had calmed down somewhat, and he rubbed me down and cleaned my feet. He was just starting home when the footman came down to the stable to say that the master wanted to see Joe. There was a man brought up for ill-using horses, and Joe's testimony was needed.

The boy stood up straight and said, "If they want evidence, they'll have it."

Master was one of the magistrates in the district, so they had brought the case before him. It was probably an hour before Joe came back, and when he did, he came into my stall and gave me a good-natured slap.

"We showed them, didn't we, Beauty? We won't see that fellow around for awhile, will we?"

We heard later that Joe's words and the marks on the horses were enough to send the man to prison for possibly two or three months.

And what a change this made in Joe. I won't call him Little Joe any more. Though he was still gentle and kind, he didn't seem like a boy anymore. To me, he was more like a grown man.

CHAPTER 7

I Leave Birtwick

I had lived at Birtwick three happy years, and would have been glad to live here forever, but it was not to be. The Doctor had been coming often to see our mistress, and lately master looked sad all the time.

Then we heard that our mistress needed a warm climate. She would have to leave England. Such sad, heavy news.

Birtwick would be sold. Master and mistress leaving. What would happen to us?

John was solemn these days, and Joe seldom whistled as he used to do. Ginger and I had a lot of work to do as our master made his preparations for the move.

Soon we learned what the arrangements were for us. Ginger and I had been sold to the master's friend, Lord William, Earl of Worcester. Merrylegs was given to the vicar, and Joe would go to the vicar's to work for him. When I heard that, I thought Merrylegs was well off.

John had several offers for jobs, but turned each one down. He said he wanted to be sure and find a good place.

Miss Jessie and Flora, with their governess, left first. When they came to tell us good-bye, it was so sad. The girls kept hugging poor Merrylegs until it was time to go, and cried when they left.

Merrylegs felt like crying, too.

The last evening, master came into the stable and went around to each of us. I could tell by his voice that he was feeling low.

"Have you decided what to do, John?" he asked. "You still haven't accepted a position, have you?"

"No, sir. Not yet. I'm hoping to find a job as a horse trainer or colt breaker. I've seen horses who had bad treatment, and I know I can do better, so I'm looking for a place where I can help get them off to a good start."

"I wish I knew of a place like that," said master. Then he added, "I will recommend you to my agent in London. Perhaps he can help."

The time came, finally, for master to go. He thanked John for his long and faithful service, but that was too much for John.

"Please, sir," John said. "Don't say anything. You and mistress have done more for me than I could ever repay. I'll never forget you, sir. May God bring you back to us, and may God make mistress well again."

Master gave John his hand, not saying anything, and then left.

Ginger and I pulled the carriage up to the Hall door for the last time. The servants brought out cushions and bedding to make a place for mistress, and when all was ready, master came down the steps carrying her in his arms and laid her in the carriage on the bed they had made. The servants were all crying.

"Good-bye again," master told them. "We shall not forget any of you." And he got in. "Let's go, John."

When we reached the railway station, master helped mistress to the waiting room, and I

heard her say to John, "Good-bye, John. God bless you."

John didn't answer her. I doubt if he could speak. The train came, and a few minutes later pulled away from the station. We watched till they were out of sight.

"We shall never see her again," John said sadly. "Never." He took the reins and we drove slowly home.

Or, rather, what we used to call home.

We parted the next morning after breakfast. Merrylegs and Joe went to the vicar. Before they left, Joe came to say good-bye. Merrylegs, out in the yard waiting, neighed to us while Joe gave rubbed our noses and gave us pats.

John took Ginger and me to Earl's Manor, or Earlshall Park, as it was called. It was only about fifteen miles, but it seemed a long way to me.

The house was fine, at least, and the stables were clean. Maybe this would be a good place.

We went through a stone gateway into the yard, and John asked for Mr. York, the coachman. It took a while before he came.

I liked Mr. York's appearance, but he seemed a bit bossy.

Ginger and I were taken to a nice stable with enough windows to give plenty of light, and placed in boxes next to each other. The grooms rubbed us down and fed us. It was probably half an hour before Mr. York came back, and John was with him.

"Now, Mr. Manly," he said, "I don't see anything obviously wrong with these horses, but it pays to be careful. Would you say they have any peculiarities I need to know about?"

"Well, sir," John told him, "I don't believe there is a better pair of horses in the country. It pains me to part with them.

"The black one is the most even-tempered horse I've ever known. I don't suppose he has ever heard a harsh word or had a rough blow since he was foaled.

"The chestnut was mistreated before we bought her. The dealer told us about it, and you can tell from her manner sometimes. She can be irritable: flies bother her; sharp noises bother her; little things like that. If she's treated well, she's strong and a good worker. But if someone were mean to her, I imagine she could be hard to handle."

York nodded. "I see. Well, we'll do what we can with her."

The two men were leaving when John thought of something else. "I might mention that we have never used the bearing rein with either of these animals. The black horse has never worn one, and the dealer said it was the bearing rein that spoiled the chestnut's temper."

"Uh, oh," York said. "They'll have to get used to it here. Both his lordship and I prefer the loose rein, but his wife, it's another thing. She thinks the bearing rein makes a carriage horse look stylish."

John shook his head. "I don't like to hear that." Then he looked at his watch. "I must go, or I'll miss my train."

He came round to each of us on his way out. I said good-bye as best I could, then he was gone.

CHAPTER 8

Her Ladyship Gets Her Way

The next day Lord William came to look at Ginger and me.

"Yes," he told York, "two fine horses. They'll do fine."

When York told him what John had said about the bearing rein, he said that he would start with the reins loose and increase them gradually.

"I'll speak to her ladyship," he promised.

We began that afternoon. Ginger and I were hitched to the carriage and driven round to the front. Lord William's mansion was twice the size of Birtwick, maybe larger.

We didn't have footmen at Birtwick, yet here were two of them, stiff and proper in their uniforms. When her ladyship descended the stairs, I heard the rustle of silk.

I couldn't turn to look at her, though. My head was pulled back so I could only see straight ahead. This was my first time of wearing a bearing rein. How would Ginger take this?

The next afternoon we were again hitched to the carriage. When her ladyship came out, I heard the swish of her silk dress, and heard something else, too.

"Put those heads higher, York." Our mistress at Birtwick would never use such a tone. "Get them up where they belong."

York gave a little nod and touched his cap. When he spoke, he selected his words carefully. "Forgive me, my lady, but these horses have not had the checkrein for three years, and my lord suggested I bring their heads up a little at a time."

"I said I want them higher," her ladyship demanded. "They may as well get used to it now."

York nodded again. "Yes, ma'am." He came around to our heads and shortened the rein one hole, and I began to understand what I had heard about the bearing rein.

So long as the road was level it wasn't too bad, but when we came to a steep hill, it was impossible. Had I been able to put my head forward, I could have easily taken the carriage up the hill.

But now I had two bits in my mouth, and the reins from the second one were pulled back and fastened to the saddle. It was bad enough when the ground was even, but with my head tied, I had no strength. When I tried to pull, it strained my back and legs.

Later, back at the stables, Ginger told me, "See what I mean? And if you think this was bad.... Today it was only one hole shorter. Wait till they make it two or three."

Three o'clock the next day. Out again. With that checkrein getting tighter. My neck ached even before I was hitched up, and my mouth and my tongue hurt. Instead of looking forward to going out, I began to dread it.

One afternoon her ladyship was late, and her temper was shorter than ever.

"To the Dutchess' house," she ordered York. Then, "When are you going to get those horses' heads up? I want them up, and now."

York nodded and touched his cap. "Yes, ma'am."

He came to me first, while the groom stood by Ginger. He pulled the rein so tight I could barely stand it. Ginger was already tossing her head; she knew what was coming.

York had to loosen the rein before he could tighten it, and the moment Ginger had her chance, she took it, and reared up so suddenly that she bumped York's face and knocked his cap off, nearly trampling the groom.

Both York and the groom grabbed for her reins, but Ginger reared again.

She even kicked me, though she didn't mean to, and kicked over the carriage pole and fell to the ground, where she still struggled against being restrained.

York grabbed Ginger's head, holding her down as he yelled to the groom: "Unbuckle the black horse. Cut the traces. Here, somebody help us."

Minutes later I was freed and led to my box. My leg hurt where Ginger had kicked, but I couldn't get my head around to look at it. That awful bearing rein still pulled at my head.

My leg pained me. I was angry at being misused. I was angry at what was happening to Ginger. To tell the truth, I was miserable.

Ginger was in bad shape when they brought her in. York barked out his orders and then came to check me over. The first thing he did was to release the pull on my head.

"Blast these bearing reins," he said under his breath. "Shows how much my lady listens. What if she missed the Duchess' party. Her own fault, I say."

York was careful to keep his words to himself; he didn't want his boss to hear. Or worse, the boss's wife.

York felt me all over, and when he found the place where I had been kicked, he grumbled some more.

Ginger never had to pull the carriage again, but when her bruises had healed, one of his Lordship's sons said he wanted her to hunt with.

I still had to pull the carriage, with that hated bearing rein. My partner now was another black horse, Max. I asked him how he liked the tight rein.

"I endure it because I have to," he told me. "It is shortening my life, and it will shorten yours. But what can we do?"

93

"Don't our masters know how it hurts us?"
I asked.

"Who can say?" Max answered. "But the
dealers and the vets know. A dealer who was
training me told one of his men that unless he
used a tight rein, no one would buy his horses.
He said London people want their horses to
step high and carry their heads high. Maybe
it's bad for horses, but it's good for trade. The
sooner the horse wears out or gets sick, the
sooner a dealer can sell another one."

Max's words didn't make me feel any better. The next four months with that rein were
bad ones for me. I wonder, if it had continued
much longer, would I have been able to stand
it? Or would I have done what Ginger did?

CHAPTER 9

Lady Anne

Relief came for me in early spring, when Lord William took part of the family to London. Ginger and I stayed at Earlshall Park.

Lady Harriet, the mistress' mother, was not able to be out, and she stayed at the mansion.

So did Lord George, the master's son, and one of his daughters, Lady Anne. She was young and energetic and liked to ride. Lady Anne called me "Black Auster," and usually chose me. I enjoyed these outings in the cool spring air.

Sometimes her brother or her cousins went along, riding Ginger or Lizzie. Lizzie was a good horse, but was high spirited and unpredictable.

One of the cousins named Blantyre was a guest at the Hall. Lizzie was his favorite mount. In fact, he liked Lizzie so much that one day Lady Anne asked that her saddle be put on Lizzie and the other saddle on me.

Blantyre was puzzled. "Don't you like Black Auster anymore?"

"It's not that," Anne replied. "It's just that after all you've said about Lizzie, I want to try her for once."

"Well, be careful," Blantyre told her, "Lizzie can be a handful."

"Oh, hush," Lady Anne laughed. "I can take care of myself. I learned to ride when I was a child. I've ridden with the hounds many times on the hunt. Just watch me ride Lizzie."

Finally, Blantyre gave in and helped Lady Anne into the saddle. Just as we were leaving, a servant came out with a slip of paper from Lady Harriet.

"Would you give this message to the Doctor," he asked. "Ask if he would send back a note with his answer."

It didn't take long to get to the Doctor's house, which set back from the road in a grove of trees. As Blantyre dismounted, Lady Anne said that she would wait outside.

"There's no need for me to go in. I'll wait here."

Across the road was a big field, and a boy with several horses.

Blantyre looped my rein over one of the spikes on the gate and disappeared in the trees between us and the house. It wasn't far. He was close enough that we could hear him knock when he reached the front door.

Lady Anne waited, enjoying the air and the peaceful surroundings. I noticed that the boy in the field had a whip in his hand, and while we watched, he started driving the horses in our direction.

Maybe he didn't see the open gate. All at once one of the colts bolted across the road toward us. The boy yelled and cracked his whip again.

Startled, Lizzie reared and took off at a gallop, nearly throwing Lady Anne, who grabbed Lizzie's mane and tried to hang on.

I neighed to sound the alarm. I neighed again and stamped my foot; anything to get Blantyre's attention. All this time Lizzie was tearing down the road with Lady Anne holding on for dear life.

Suddenly Blantyre came running from the house and saw what was happening: Lady Anne was a good ways off by now, with Lizzie still in full gallop. In an instant Blantyre was in the saddle and we went after them.

The road ran straight, then curved to the right, then divided into two roads. By the time we came to the bend, Lady Anne was nowhere to be seen. Had it not been for an old woman working in her garden, we might have taken the wrong road.

Blantyre slowed and shouted, "Which way?"

"To the right," the woman yelled, pointing to the right.

Moments later we caught sight of the runaway, then lost her, then caught another glimpse, and she was gone again.

Farther on we came upon a workman, who directed us, "To the common, sir."

The common field was a poor place to ride a horse very fast, being rough and covered with scrub bushes and with hardly a grassy spot anywhere.

We saw them now.

Lady Anne's hair was streaming out behind her. Even from this distance we could see that she was pulling at the reins, trying to get Lizzie to slop.

Lizzie had slowed, so we gained a little, but they were still far ahead.

Someone had recently dug an open ditch across the common, with the dirt still piled up on the far side of the cut. Rather than stop, Lizzie took the leap.

But she didn't make it and fell hard. Poor Lady Anne was thrown to the ground.

"Oh, no," said Blantyre, as we closed the distance between us and the ditch. Giving me a free rein, he whispered, "Now, Auster, do your best."

Doing my utmost, I cleared both the ditch and the bank of dirt.

Poor Lady Anne lay motionless in the dirt. Blantyre knelt down and spoke her name. Nothing.

Carefully he wiped the dirt away from her face and kept saying her name. "Annie; it's me. Say something, Annie."

Two men who had seen the runaway horse and had tried to follow came to us. "Is she hurt? What can we do?" one of them asked.

"Take my horse"—Blantyre pointed to me— "and go to the Doctor. Bring him at once. Then go to Earlshall and ask them to bring the carriage and Lady Anne's maidservant. I'll stay here."

It was done. One man ran for some water. The other jumped into the saddle and dug his heels into my sides and off we went.

He guided me around the ditch, which delayed us a bit, and he acted as if he wished he had a whip. My pace soon cured him of that notion. As fast as I was going, the best thing he could do was to stick to the saddle and let me run.

At the doctor's they asked him in for a drink, but he told them no, and we headed toward Earlshall.

You can imagine the excitement when the household heard the news. I was taken to my box, where they removed the saddle and bridle and threw a blanket over me. Ginger was saddled and sent off in a hurry. Minutes later I heard the carriage roll out.

It seemed a long time later before Ginger came back and told me what happened.

"I got there," Ginger told me, "just as the Doctor arrived. There was a little crowd of

people around Lady Anne, and a woman was holding the Lady's head in her lap. The Doctor gave Lady Anne a dose of something, and I heard him say, 'She's not dead.'

"Then a man led me off to the side and I just stood there. The carriage came in a few minutes, and the men lifted Lady Anne up, carefully, so carefully, and we came home together."

I noticed that Ginger coughed now and then as she talked. She didn't complain, but it worried me.

A couple of days after the accident, Blantyre came to check on me. He patted me and kept telling Lord George that he was sure I knew Anne's danger as well as he did.

"I could not have reined him in if I wanted to," he said. "Lady Anne should stick to Black Auster."

That sounded good. Maybe Lady Anne was out of danger and we could go riding before long.

CHAPTER 10

Troubles, Troubles, Troubles

It's not often that a person can do wrong without hurting himself and others as well. That's the way it was with Reuben Smith, who was left in charge of the stables when York went to London with his lordship.

Reuben was good with horses. He had worked for two years with a veterinarian, and was as good as any horse doctor. He was strong, and likeable, and could drive four horses as easily as most drivers could manage a pair.

I heard two grooms talking one time, wondering why Reuben was in a second place job rather than being in charge. I had wondered that myself.

Then Max found out the reason: Reuben liked to drink. Not like some men. He didn't drink all the time. No, for months Reuben would stay sober and never touch a drop. Then he would lose control, take a drink, and end up embarrassing himself and making life miserable for his wife and children.

But he was such a good worker that more than once York kept quiet and said nothing to his lordship. The Earl might never have known, except that one night Reuben was too drunk to drive some of the Earl's party guests home.

Reuben was fired, of course. But he came back and begged York, and begged the Earl, and his Lordship gave him one more chance.

Reuben knew how close he had come, and he stayed off the bottle so well that York began to think Reuben was cured.

It was now early April, and the family was expected home in May. Reuben had an errand in town, so he saddled me up and we went.

Usually we came straight home, but this time Reuben stopped at a pub and ordered the attendant to feed me and have me ready by four o'clock.

A nail in one of my front shoes had started to loosen, and the groom did not notice the problem until nearly four. Reuben was late, and when he finally came, the groom told Reuben about the nail and asked if he wanted it taken care of.

"I don't have time," Reuben snapped. "It can wait till we get home."

I had never heard Reuben speak that way before. Then he went back inside the White Lion. What was wrong, I wondered.

It was close to nine when he finally came for me and we started home. I had never seen him in such an ugly humor.

The moon was not out yet, and the road was so dark I could hardly see. This was no night to go fast, but Reuben laid into me with his whip and made me gallop despite the darkness. I could feel my shoe coming loose, and it came off when we were about halfway home.

If he hadn't been so drunk, Reuben would have known something was wrong. I managed until we came to a stony section; some of those stones were sharp. Oblivious to my discomfort, Reuben pressed me to go all out, hitting me constantly with his whip and cursing and yelling for me to go even faster.

Within minutes my foot was cut. Minutes more, and my hoof was split down to the very quick and becoming worse.

I couldn't stand it. I stumbled and fell, and Reuben was thrown. He hit hard. We had been moving right along.

It took me a couple of tries and considerable pain, but I scrambled to my feet and stood there waiting for him to get up, but he did not move. There was a heavy groan, and then he was still.

I could have groaned, too, from the pain of my knees and my foot. But horses bear their pain in silence, so I stood and waited, keeping my weight off the injured hoof.

In the silence I could hear the wind whisper through the new leaves, but nothing else. After a while the moon came out. Nothing moved except the clouds, and a brown owl making its silent way.

Around midnight I heard a sound off in the distance. There; I heard it again, faint and far away, but it sounded like a horse.

If only it was someone looking for us.

The sound came nearer, and I realized it was Ginger, pulling the dog-cart.

I neighed loudly. Ginger neighed back, and then I heard men's voices. Someone was coming, finally.

They stopped at the dark form still lying on the ground.

"It's Reuben," said one of the men. "He looks like he's dead to me."

"Oh, my," said the other, getting down and bending over the still figure. "Yes, he's dead. A good while, too. Feel how cold his hands are."

They raised up the body, but there was no life. Even in the dim light I could see that his hair was soaked in blood. They laid him down again and came to look at me.

When they touched my knee, I winced. "Look at these knees," one of them, a man named Robert, said. "This horse has fallen, and that's why Smith got thrown. Why, I never knew this one to throw a rider, ever."

He tried to lead me forward, but I could only make one step, and almost fell again.

"This horse is hurt," Robert said. "His hoof is all cut up! The shoe is gone. Ned, do you smell the booze? He's drunk, or was—he's dead, now—and I'll bet he was going at a good clip. Over these stones, too. With no shoe. No wonder the horse fell."

The man called Ned walked over to Smith's body. "You killed yourself, Reuben, do you know that? You hurt your horse and you killed yourself."

The two men loaded the body onto the cart and Ned drove it away. Robert led me the three miles to home.

Robert tried to be careful. He could tell I was in pain. He took his handkerchief and bandaged my foot but it still hurt. He walked slowly and tried to be gentle, but the trip home was a painful one for me.

At last I was home and in my own box. I didn't eat much, and barely slept. When the farrier came, he said he hoped I was not spoiled for work.

Yes; it was a bad night for me. It was much worse for Reuben's family. After the funeral his wife had to move out of the coach house. Her husband was dead, her children were fatherless, and where was she going to live?

My knees finally healed enough that I could be outside, and I was put out into a field to recover from my injuries. I had the field to

myself, and was glad for this chance to get my strength back.

Imagine my surprise when one morning the gate opened and Ginger was let in. I let out a whinny and trotted over to see her. It was great to be together again.

Over the next few days Ginger told me bits and pieces of why she had been put out in the field, too. It was not a pretty story.

Lord George was young, heavy, and headstrong. No one could tell him anything. He would hunt whenever he got a chance, whether there was work for him to do or not. And when he hunted, he could be hard on his horse.

Soon after I left the stable there was a steeplechase, and George was determined to ride. He wanted to use Ginger, but the groom told him that she was not ready. George didn't care and took her anyway. With her high spirits, Ginger did her utmost to keep up with the other horses and came in among the first three. But her wind was gone and his weight had strained her back.

In fact, Ginger was in such bad condition that the groom turned her out into the field where I was.

"Here we are," she said to me, "both of us with problems; you with your knees and fore-foot, and I with my back and lungs."

Sadly, she was right. I wasn't the horse I used to be, and neither was Ginger. Even here in the field where we could do whatever we wanted, we never ran if we could walk. We didn't have the energy. How could we ever work again?

When the Earl came back from London, he and York came to look us over. I didn't like what I saw on master's face.

"Three hundred pounds thrown away for no good reason," he complained. "But even worse than the money is that two horses, good horses when they came to me, are ruined now. I can keep the mare for a year, perhaps, but no more; but the black one must go. With knees all scarred like that, the mistress would never permit him to be seen in public."

When they turned to go, Ginger and I stood there and watched till they were gone. I couldn't speak, and it was a while before she did.

"They're going to sell you," said Ginger, "and I'll lose the only friend I ever had. We'll never see each other again."

I didn't say anything.

I couldn't.

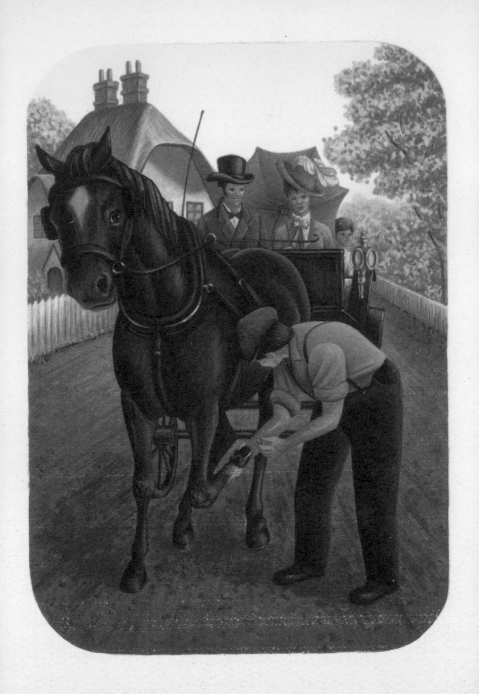

CHAPTER 11

I Become a Job Horse

York recommended me to someone he knew who managed a livery stable. This gave me my first train ride.

That was some experience; the noise of the engine and whistle, being put into a narrow box, feeling the jerks and shaking of the train car as it moved away, trying to keep my footing and not fall.

But it did me no harm, and at the end of the train ride I was taken to a fairly comfortable stable, though these were not so airy and pleasant as the ones I had at Earlshall.

I was used to stalls which were built on level ground, but these were laid on a slope.

The groom kept me tied to the manger, so I was never able to stand on level ground, which was hard on my back and my legs.

I wish men would realize that horses could do more work if they were able to move around and have a comfortable stall. I'm not complaining. Here they fed me well. The place was clean. My new owner gave us as good care as he could, considering how busy he was and how many horses he had to look after.

His business was to hire out carriages. He owned the horses and the carriages, and had drivers working for him.

He also had several carriages which he would rent to people who wanted to drive themselves. Once in awhile, even a lady would rent one of us.

All this was new to me. Before now I had always been driven by people who knew how to drive. Now it was different. I was a "job-horse." That is, I was let out to anyone who wanted to hire me. It didn't matter whether or not they could drive, or whether they were gentle or harsh.

In fact, since I was so even tempered, I have an idea that my new master let me go with drivers who were not so good, because he knew he could rely on me.

You can imagine some of the experiences I had. For example, I had some really bad drivers.

First, there were the tight-rein kind. Their idea of driving a horse was to keep pulling hard on the rein all the time. They never relaxed their pull on the horse's mouth or gave him any freedom of movement.

These people always talk about "keeping the horse well in hand" or "holding his head up," as if a horse didn't know how to hold his own head up!

The opposite kind are the loose-rein drivers. They don't even hold the reins, letting them lie slack across our backs. The horse never quite knows what is expected of him.

121

These people have no control over a horse. If the horse stumbles, or if something startles him, the driver can't help the horse at all. By the time the loose-rein type gets things in hand, it may be too late.

While I preferred the loose-rein types to the tight-rein drivers, a horse likes to have some help, especially when he's going downhill.

Plus, a horse likes to know the driver's not asleep!

Poor driving is bad for horses. A horse can become lazy or can learn bad habits. Squire Gordon always said it was as bad to spoil a horse as it was to spoil a child, and both had to suffer for it later on.

Then there are drivers who are just plain careless. One day I went out with a driver who had a lady and two children with him. He flopped the reins all over the place when we started, and I thought, "Uh, oh." He gave me several nasty cuts with the whip to make me go along rather fast.

But that wasn't all. Here I am running down the road and he is back there laughing and joking with the lady and the children, paying no attention to the road or to me.

We came to a place where workmen were mending the road, but my driver never noticed. Nor did he notice when I picked up a stone in my shoe.

If Mr. Gordon, or if John, or if any good driver had been there, he would have seen

before we had gone three paces that something was wrong. But not this fellow.

He drove me with that stone in my foot—digging in further at every step—for half a mile before he even noticed. By then the pain was so bad I had to slow down. I could hardly put my foot to the ground.

Now he saw it. "Well! Here's one for you! They've sent us out with a lame horse. What a shame."

He then slapped me with the reins and took the whip to me and said, "No use playing games with us. We're going on and you're going to take us."

I was surely glad when a farmer rode up and interrupted. "I beg your pardon, sir," he said, "but I think there's something wrong with his shoe. I wouldn't be surprised if he has picked up a stone, from the way he's limping. I'll take a look if you would like."

"That's fine with me," my driver answered. "He's hired, and I don't know anything about him."

The farmer got down and picked up my forefoot. "I say, no wonder he's gone lame. There is a stone here."

The farmer first tried to remove the stone with his fingers, but it was wedged too tightly. So he took a stonepick out of his pocket and worked and worked until he had it out.

"There," he said, showing the stone to the driver, "that's the stone your horse picked up. It's a wonder he didn't fall and break his knees."

"Of all things!" answered the driver. "I didn't know horses got stones in their shoes."

The farmer could have said something sharp, but he did not. "Well, my friend, you do now. Even a good horse can pick up a stone. And when it does, you'll want to get it out right away."

After the farmer left, my driver slapped me with the reins again, and I had to go on. At least the stone was out.

Another kind of driver is the steam-engine type. This kind were usually from the city, or a town, and had never been around animals or owned a horse of their own.

These people seemed to think a horse was just another engine. Maybe a little smaller. Maybe needing grass instead of fuel. But just another engine.

If you have a job to do, a place to go, or a load to move, hitch a horse to it and pull away. Uphill or down. Smooth roads or rough. Bad

weather or good. No difference; just hitch up the horse and pull.

Would these people think of getting out when going up a hill? Not at all. They've paid to ride and they're going to ride. If the load is heavy, whip the horse harder.

If I had a choice, I would rather go twenty miles with a driver who is considerate than half that far with one of these. I wouldn't wear out so fast.

What's even worse is that these drivers never put on the drag-brake, no matter how steep the hill is. Or, if they do remember to put it on, they forget to take it off at the bottom. It's no fun straining everything you have and be halfway up a hill before the driver realizes he has the drag on.

Some drivers must think they're racers or something. Rather than starting off at a nice, easy pace, they go full speed from the first. When they want to stop, they yank the rein and tear at the horse's mouth. And when they

Black Beauty

turn a corner, they pay no attention to staying on their own side of the road.

One time I was out with a horse named Rory. Our driver was a good one, and even though we had worked all day, it had been pleasant. On the way back we were coming to an intersection when it happened.

As we neared the corner, I couldn't see anything for the high hedge, but I could hear another rig coming along rapidly. The next moment he was upon us.

I was on the side near the hedge, but not poor Rory. The rig crashed into Rory and the shaft went right into his chest. I'll never forget the sound he made.

The oncoming horse was knocked down, too, and the gig was all broken. It turned out that it was a horse from one of our own stables, so I learned the full story later.

The driver was the kind who think they know it all. Even after the accident, it didn't bother him to see what he had done to Rory.

To him, Rory didn't matter. All that mattered to the driver was that he would be late.

If that driver had been over on our side just a little bit farther, he might have killed Rory. Maybe that would have been better, because it took Rory's wounds a long time to heal, and when he did get better, the master sold him to a coal dealer. If there's a worse job, I don't know what it would be, dragging a coal wagon up and down hills in all kinds of weather.

Maybe I sound as if we only had bad experiences, but that isn't so. One special memory for me is the time I was driven to a house on Pulteny Street.

Two gentlemen climbed into the gig, and the one who drove had such a good touch with the reins. What pleasure to have a good driver. I held my head up and trotted off just like old times. The driver liked me as well as I liked him, and that's how it came that I was sold to Mr. Barry.

CHAPTER 12

New Owner, New Problems

My new master was not married. He lived in the city of Bath, and was deeply involved in many business ventures. His doctor told him he should find something to do outside, and he decided to buy a horse. So he bought me.

There was a stable close to where he lived. He put me there, and hired a groom named Filcher.

My new master didn't know much about horses. He was good to me though, and ordered good quality feed for me. Everything went fine for a while.

Filcher kept things clean. He was a good groom. He liked to work in his garden, and kept rabbits and chickens to sell.

It wasn't long before I noticed that I wasn't getting as much oats as I did at first. I was still fed the beans, but there was bran mixed with them instead of oats. I started to feel the difference in my strength and my spirits. I needed more than grass to keep up my strength. Did the master know what was happening?

One afternoon master took me to see a farmer who lived near the town of Wells. As soon as he saw me, master's friend spoke up.

"What's wrong with your horse?" he asked. "He looked better when you first bought him. He's not sick, is he?"

"My groom says he's fine," answered my master, "and that it's normal for a horse to be less active in the autumn."

"Nuts to that," said the farmer. "There is something wrong with that horse. I can tell. What kind of food are you giving him?"

"Only the best," my master explained, and told how he had bought exactly what the dealer had recommended.

The other man didn't answer immediately, but looked me over and felt my coat and my shoulders. When he spoke, he was deeply serious. "I would not accuse anyone, but I would say that this horse is not getting what you say you are buying for him."

Had I been able to speak, I could have told master where his oats had been going all along. Every morning before daylight Filcher would bring his little boy to the stable, and the boy carried a covered basket. Filcher would take his son into the feed room and pour some of my oats into the boy's basket and the boy would leave.

One morning about a week after our visit to master's friend, Filcher and his boy came in as usual, but this time a policeman was waiting and caught them. I was glad to be rid of Filcher, but his replacement was even worse.

My new groom's name was Alfred Smirk. He was the biggest cheat I ever knew.

Al was always very good when master was around, stroking and petting me. When master wanted me to take him somewhere, Al always brushed my mane and my tail with water and my hoofs with oil to make me look good.

But when it came to cleaning my feet or taking care of my shoes, or grooming my coat the way it should be done — he was a total fraud. I've seen cows who were treated better than I was. My bit became rusty, but he didn't care. He let my saddle get damp, and my crupper stiff.

Al put a little mirror up in the harness-room, and every time he passed that mirror, he stopped and checked his hair and brushed it back.

He could say "Yes, sir," and "No, sir," but he couldn't work. Or at least, he did not work. Not when he could get out of it.

My stall, for example. I had a loose box, and it would have been nice, but the straw

was filthy. Instead of cleaning out the stable as he should, Al would throw down a layer of fresh straw on top and do nothing about what was underneath.

The smell made my eyes burn. I didn't even want to eat.

Master spoke to Al and suggested that he clean the stable, but Al had an answer for him. "Sir," he began, "I'll do whatever you ask, but remember that you must not splash water around a horse's box. You wouldn't want him to take cold. I would not want to harm such a fine animal."

If only I could speak!

My straw was so wet already, and filthy besides, that my feet became infected.

I don't think Al would have ever done anything. One day when master was riding me, my feet hurt so badly that I stumbled twice and nearly threw him. On the way home he stopped to ask the farrier to look at me.

It didn't take the farrier long to find out. "It's the 'thrush,'" he told Mr. Barry. "Your horse has a bad case. We usually find this kind in stables which are not cleaned properly. Has your groom seen this? Send him over tomorrow, and I'll give him instructions so we can cure your horse."

Finally, I had my feet properly treated and my stable cleaned the way they should be. But if the farrier had not been there, Alfred would never have done it right.

Maybe things will be better now, I thought, but no. It wasn't to be. Mr. Barry, having been cheated by two grooms, decided he would get rid of me and hire a horse if he needed one.

So I was to be sold again.

CHAPTER 13

Another New Home

Have you ever seen a horse fair? You would probably like it. There you can see big horses, work horses, fancy horses—all kinds of horses.

You might see shaggy little Welsh ponies about the size of Merrylegs. Or cart horses, some with their tails braided and tied with ribbons, some a lot like me, well bred and strong, but now considered second class due to an accident or fault.

You would see many beautiful horses, still in their prime, but on sale for some reason.

Out back will be the sad ones, broken down by hard work and careless owners. Poor animals; their knees crooked, their hind legs stiff and awkward.

Some are merely old, lips hanging and eyes dull. Looking at them, I always wonder if I will look like them someday.

There is always a lot of excitement at a horse fair; people running here and there, making offers, buying and selling. There are a lot of lies told at a horse fair, you can be sure.

They put me with an assortment of still healthy and useful animals and many people stopped to look us over. Once they saw my knees, though, most buyers turned away. The man selling me swore it was only a slip in my stall, but unfortunately no one wants a horse which can't stand up.

A few did take time for a longer look. They looked in my mouth, looked at my eyes, felt my coat and my legs, and made me try my paces.

What a difference in people. Some treated me like I was a piece of wood. Others were easy as they patted my coat or rubbed my legs and sides. While the buyers were judging me, I was judging them.

There was one man I wished would buy me. He didn't look like a rich man, but he knew horses. His eyes were grey, his hands were small. In fact, the man himself was not very big. He was quick, yet gentle. When he spoke, his voice was not harsh.

It may sound funny, but the first thing I noticed was the smell of him—it was like the outdoors, not of stale beer and tobacco. It was a fresh smell as if he had just come from a hayloft.

He offered twenty-three pounds for me, but the dealer turned him down. I was sorry to see him walk away.

A hard-looking man came, and I thought, oh, no; I don't want you to buy me. But he walked on, and I was relieved.

Others came and made offers, but no one seemed to mean business.

141

The hard faced man came back and offered twenty-three pounds. He and my seller argued, and I thought I was a goner. But then the grey-eyed man came back. I reached out my face and he stroked my nose.

"Say, old fellow," he said, "you and I might make a team, do you think?"

"Make it twenty-five and he's yours," said the seller.

"Twenty-four ten," said my friend. "Twenty-four ten and that's tops. Is it a deal?"

"A deal!" said the seller. "And if I may say so, he'll make a good cab horse."

My new owner counted out the money and took his receipt. I was led out of there and taken to a nearby inn, where he saddled me and gave me some oats. He was good company while I ate, talking to himself and talking to me.

Within half an hour we were on our way, passing through towns and traveling country roads until we came to the highway leading into London.

We reached the city at dusk, our way lit by gaslight. So many streets, crossing each other for mile upon mile. I thought they must go on forever.

At last we turned up a side street, then into a narrow alley. There were some run-down houses on one side and what I supposed were coach-houses and stables on the other.

My owner gave a sharp whistle and a door flew open and out came a young mother, followed by a little girl and a boy.

"Harry," said my owner, "open the stable gates while your mother gets the lantern."

Everyone stood around me, talking all at once.

"Is he gentle, father?"

"Yes, Dolly. Come and pat him."

How nice to have that little hand rubbing my shoulder and neck.

"I'll fix a mash for him while you rub him down," the mother said.

"He's ready for it, Polly. He's had a long ride."

Jeremiah Barker was my new master's name, but everybody called him Jerry. His wife's name was Polly, and the children were Harry, twelve, and Dorothy, or Dolly as they called her, eight.

Such a happy family! They were good to each other and good to me. I knew I would enjoy being here.

Jerry was a cab driver, one of the thousands in London. His cab looked like all the others, with the driver's box out front in the weather and the lamps on either side, and the big rear wheels. Jerry owned his cab, and he kept it clean and in good shape. People liked to ride with Jerry.

His other horse was a big white animal named Captain, the kind of horse you see in pictures of war heroes. In fact, Captain had been in the Crimean War, and I'll tell you about that later. Captain was old now, but I have the idea that Captain was a noble animal when he was young. You could see it in the way he carried his head, and in the way he stepped.

The morning after I came to Jerry's, he groomed me and then mother and daughter came to see me and get acquainted. Polly had a slice of apple for me, and Dolly brought me a piece of bread. What a wonderful way to begin life in my new home. I could even take hard cab work, if I were treated like this when I came home.

Looking at me, Polly told her husband, "He's too fine for a cab horse."

"Well," Jerry said, "if his knees weren't all scarred up, he wouldn't be here."

"Wonder how it happened?" she asked.

"The dealer didn't say," Jerry answered. "It doesn't worry me. I'll take him out and we'll see how it goes. What do you want to name him? Should we call him 'Jack,' too?"

"Yes," Polly said. "I liked the old Jack, and let's keep the same name for this one."

Jerry took Captain out all morning, and I stayed by myself. After school Harry came to give me water and feed. All day I kept wondering what working as a cab horse would be like, and was a little nervous when Jerry came for me in the late afternoon.

Jerry took care with my collar and bridle so that they fit, and didn't rub me the wrong way. He was so considerate that he reminded

me of John Manley. He even fixed the crupper so that it wasn't too bad.

Great! There was no bearing rein. My head was free.

Jerry worked at a cab stand on one of London's main thoroughfares. It was a good location, and did a lot of business. There was a constant stream of traffic up and down the avenue, and people came all through the day and evening to the stand, needing a cab to take them somewhere.

Across the street were tall row houses, with storefronts on the street level and residences above. On our side was an old church and a small churchyard, enclosed by an iron rail fence, and our stand was alongside this fence.

Some of the drivers were standing and talking, one or two were giving their horses water or hay, another was sitting on the driver's box of his cab, reading a newspaper, oblivious to the noise of the street.

Jerry pulled our cab up at the end of the line. Seeing the new horse, several drivers came around to look me over.

"As black as he is, you could keep him for funerals," one of them suggested.

"Too good a horse for that," said another. Then, seeing my knees, he shook his head. "That one's got a bad fault hidden somewhere, or I'll miss my guess."

Jerry laughed. "I needn't find trouble till trouble finds me. Let me think I've got a good one for a while longer, at least."

A big man who seemed to be in charge came up then, and the others made way for him. His hat was gray, and his coat was gray with white buttons. He had a blue scarf around his neck. His hair was gray, too, as if it were part of his uniform.

The men called him "Governor," but his name was Grant. Governor examined me as carefully as if he were going to buy me himself, then straightened up and told Jerry, "You've got a fine one here."

Immediately my status went up with the other drivers. If Governor said I was a fine horse, then a fine horse I was. And to be treated as such.

The men respected Governor, and let him handle any problems or disputes which arose. In addition to common sense, Governor had two big fists, and he didn't mind using them,

especially after a couple of drinks. Some of the men had bruises to remind them.

My home was good; my owner was good; but my work was hard. Especially at first.

City life was new to me. I had always lived in open spaces, with big fields where I could run, country lanes for my work, and farm life all around me.

The city, with its noise and smells and crowds, and especially the hurry up and let's go attitude everyone showed—this was new and difficult.

Even waiting on the cab stand was unpleasant. There was not one minute, from sunup to sundown and after, but that the street was crowded with wagons, carriages, riders, and other cabs. I thought often of my days in the country, with the sounds of nature, instead of this noise of wheels and horses and shouting voices.

It didn't take me long to learn that I could trust Jerry, and this helped.

He was as good a driver as I had ever had. Even better, he took as much care of his horse as he did of himself.

He soon learned I didn't need the whip, and he never used it, unless it was to touch my back with it so I knew it was time to move off. I could tell this anyway by the way he picked up the reins.

We learned to work with each other, and formed a good team. I was glad Jerry had bought me, and even though the work was hard and life in London was not easy, I was as comfortable as I could expect.

Jerry was a hard worker. He kept his stables clean. They were the old fashioned kind, built on a slope, and that was not good, but at night Jerry put bars across the back of our stalls and took off our halters so it was almost like having a loose box.

This helped me rest, and let me start my working day in good condition, which is important.

He changed our food from time to time, too. No one likes to eat the same thing day after day. There was plenty of water; clear, fresh water; all we wanted. Jerry was not like some masters, who think a horse should have only a drink now and then. How would you like to eat dry oats or hay, and no water to wash it down? I was glad for such a considerate owner.

Best of all, our new master kept his Sundays free, and let us rest. Working as hard as we did all week, if we had worked on Sundays too, I don't think we could have kept up. Besides, it was during these Sunday rest days that I learned Captain's story.

CHAPTER 14

Captain Tells His Story

C aptain had not been trained for carriage work, as I had. He had been trained as an army horse. He had to learn how to follow orders and work in formation with other horses—trotting to the right or to the left, turning with his unit, running forward with other horses, coming to a halt at the command.

In war, horses had to carry their men into battle, and a great part of Captain's training was to teach him how to go forward even when the big guns were firing, or to gallop ahead no matter the noise or commotion.

When he was young, Captain was a dappled, dark grey, and quite handsome. He was fortunate to have a young officer as his master, a man who treated Captain well and always saw to his care. Captain enjoyed parade day, when his harness was polished and his coat brushed and hooves oiled nicely. He liked the crisp orders and trumpets and flags, and took particular care to hold his head erect and step proudly.

Life in the army was exciting, and Captain liked it. That is, except for being loaded into the ship. Captain didn't like that.

"When we were sent overseas," Captain told me, "they marched us down to the dock. I could smell the salt air, and this was something new. But loading us on the ship was terrible!"

What, I wondered, could be so frightening to Captain that he would say something like that?

He went on. "One at a time they took us to the edge of the dock and then fastened big straps around us and lifted us up in the air and set us down on the ship. We were put down inside the ship in narrow stalls where we couldn't see the sky or have fresh air. They never let us out to walk, either; there was no room for it.

"When our ship went out on the water we could feel it rolling in the waves. Down where we were we couldn't tell if it was day or night. The motion bumped us against the sides of our pens. That, and the stale air, made us half sick.

"Then we landed, and once again we were strapped and lifted up in the air and swung across the water and put down on the land. How glad I was to be on solid ground!"

Captain went on to tell about the country where he had been taken.

"It was not like it is here. There were many difficulties. With so many horses and so many men, and with the war going on, supplies did not always come and sometimes our food rations were scarce.

157

"I remember the rain and the mud, and being cold. But the men did what they could for us. They had to face their hardships. War was not easy for them, either."

I asked him about the battles. "Weren't you afraid during the fighting?"

"Yes," he told me, "that could be scary, it's true. But I always liked the sound of the trumpet. It made me want to get started. Sometimes we had to stand for hours and wait. Then, when the command came we would charge forward, and we forgot about the bullets and the noise. You can't know the excitement, the feeling, unless you've been in battle yourself."

I didn't say it, but I was not much interested in finding out what being in a battle was like.

"We depended upon our riders," he told me. "When our rider was in the saddle and the reins in his hand, we were unafraid, even with shells passing overhead or exploding around us. I think I could charge right up to a cannon's mouth if my rider asked me to.

"My master and I went into action again and again, without a wound or scratch; though I saw horses shot or cut. I've seen dead horses and dying horses, and I've heard their screams. Men, too; I've seen dead men and wounded men and have heard their cries.

"But I don't think I was ever afraid for myself. If you could have known my master,

you would know why. He had a way of making me feel strong and safe. Even when he was shouting he never lost control."

Captain became silent, and I waited until he continued.

"It happened one morning in late fall. As usual, we were up before dawn. It was a dark morning, and chilly. The men stood ready by their horses, waiting for orders. Gradually it became lighter, and we could tell that the officers were excited. In the distance we could hear the firing of the big guns, then moments later, explosions when the shells landed.

"No one in our ranks said a word. Where we were the only sounds were the sounds of our breathing and the occasional stamp of a restless foot.

"An officer rode up and gave the order for the men to mount. Quickly every man was on his horse and we were ready, waiting for the signal to go. Not one of us moved yet. I watched the little clouds from my breath in the cold air.

"My master and I stood at the front, with the others behind. He ran his fingers through my mane and rubbed his hand along my neck. 'We shall be tested today,' he whispered to me. 'But we'll do our duty, we will.'

"Things happened fast after that. The order came to march, and then to gallop, and we charged across a valley right into the enemy cannon. The noise and smoke were awful, worse than anything before. To the left and right explosions ripped up huge chunks of ground, and more than once I was pelted with dirt as we rode on.

"Men fell, horses went down. Horses who had lost their riders ran here and there, terrified because they had no one to lead them.

"Despite our fear, no one held back. The closer we came to the enemy, the harder we rode. Smoke burned my nostrils and hurt my eyes. The noise was terrible.

"My master and I were still leading the rest, him cheering the others, when he was hit. I heard the bullet whiz past and felt him lurch. I tried to slow, but the rein went slack and his sword dropped and he sank backward and fell. Before I could stop, the others swept by and took me with them.

"Where was he? I was lost! I had to find him! Where to look, amidst the noise and smoke and shouting? I ran to join the others, but they beat me off. I galloped this way and then that.

"Someone grabbed my bridle and mounted and suddenly I was going forward again. It wasn't my master, though. Someone had lost his horse and took me.

"Soon the smoke lifted and the noise died away. The quiet after the battle was almost worse than the battle itself. Wounded horses lay groaning on the ground, struggling or trying to rise, or walked about, dragging one leg, or bleeding. Wounded men, too, were groaning and screaming. Others lay quiet, dead."

"Was it over then?" I asked.

"The wounded horses were not left there," Captain told me. "Army men went round the field with pistols and shot any horse badly hurt. The slightly wounded were brought back. Most of those who went out that morning never came back."

"But what happened to your master?" I wanted to know.

Captain looked away. "I never saw him again."

163

CHAPTER 15

Jerry

I've never known a better man than Jeremiah Barker. He was a good person, and always tried to do what was right. Few people could quarrel with Jerry; he was too even tempered to pick a fight. Often I could hear him humming to himself as he drove along.

The whole family helped out with the cab and with Captain and me. Harry did as much work as a much older boy. Dolly and her mother would help with the cab, cleaning the cushions and wiping the glass. Jerry groomed us while they worked on the cab, and Harry did the harness.

The only thing that irritated Jerry was when someone loafed around and wasted a lot of time, then wanted him to put pressure on his horse to make up for their laziness.

One time two fellows came out of the tavern down the street and went up to Jerry. "Hey! Victoria Station, and hurry. We've got to catch the one o'clock train. It'll mean an extra shilling if you make it."

"I'll be glad to take you," Jerry replied, "but at the usual pace. My horse is worth more than a shilling extra."

Another cab was next to ours, the horse already well used that day. The driver heard what was being said and threw open the door. "Here; I'll do it. Get in. We'll get you there." Slashing his tired horse, they disappeared into the traffic.

Jerry came around and rubbed my nose. "We're not going to run you like that, are we, Jack?"

Jerry would always go out of his way to help someone who had a genuine need.

One morning as we waited for a fare, a man carrying a heavy suitcase missed the curb and fell hard. Jerry ran and helped him up.

"Are you all right?"

The man said he was, but Jerry helped him cross the street—even carried the suitcase— to a little shop where the man could get a cup of coffee.

Ten minutes or so later, someone stepped out of the store and called across the street to Jerry: "Can you come?" So we drew up at the curb, and the man—the one who had fallen— came outside.

"Will you take me to the station?" he asked Jerry. "This has made me late, I'm afraid. I must catch the noon train, and I will be grateful if you can get me there on time."

"We'll try, sir," Jerry told him. "Are you sure you feel like going?" The man still looked pale.

"I have to. I must catch that train."

Moments later we were on our way. Driving fast in London is never easy, especially in the middle of the day. But a good driver and a good horse have the advantage if they know how to work together.

I had what they call a good mouth. It took only a touch of the rein to guide me, and when you are trying to weave your way through slow carts and heavy wagons and fast-moving carriages, and cabs picking up and letting off passengers, it makes a difference.

When you want to pass, for example, maybe an opening comes and you try to go through but the cart in front comes over and you have only inches between his wheels and yours. Or you are making good time, and you can't get around a jam-up of carts.

The driver and his horse have to be always on the watch. London has its share of bad drivers, too.

Jerry knew what I could do, and I trusted him to find the best way, so we could make good time if the need was there.

We started out with our passenger, determined to do our best. We did well until we came to Cheapside, where we had to wait in a line of stalled traffic for three or four minutes. Our passenger stuck out his head and asked, "What's wrong? Why the tie-up?"

"We'll make it," Jerry told him. "It's usually only a couple of minutes."

I could hear our passenger mumbling to himself, and I thought he might get out and try it on foot, but he stayed with us. With that suitcase, he would never make it far.

The cart in front began to move, and we were on our way again—in and out—dashing forward when we had an opening. The road was not too crowded until we came to London Bridge. It looked like every cab in London was trying to cross. Maybe they all were trying to catch that twelve o'clock train.

When we whirled into the station, the clock showed eight minutes till twelve.

"Thank you, thank you," the man said. "We are on time. Here; take this extra half-crown."

"No, thank you, sir," said Jerry. "We're glad we could help. Don't wait; you need to go. Here, porter! Take this man's luggage. The Dover line—twelve o'clock train—that's the one."

Other cabs were pulling up, and Jerry wheeled me around and out of the way.

Later, when we arrived back at the cab stand, the other drivers asked Jerry if he'd made the train.

"Yes," Jerry responded. "Jack here knows how to go, he does."

"I hope you charged him for it," Governor commented.

"Well," Jerry began, "usual fare was what I charged. He'd had enough trouble for one day. I'm glad we made it in time."

"You'll never be rich," the other driver said.

"There's more to life than money," was Jerry's answer.

One morning as Jerry was getting me ready to go, a man I recognized from the cab stand walked into the yard. "Good morning."

"Good morning, Mr. Briggs." Jerry knew this man because he often took him places.

"Jerry," he began, "Mrs. Briggs and I go to church every Sunday, and we would like to hire you to be our regular cab."

"Sir," Jerry told him, "I appreciate the offer. I really do. But for the last five years I've always kept Sunday as a day off for me and the horses."

"I see," said Mr. Briggs. "But I wonder if it would be so bad to take us to our church. It is not such a long ways, though too far for my wife to walk, and you would still have your afternoons."

"Yes, that's true," Jerry agreed. "But if I start taking fares Sunday morning, I might want to keep at it for the afternoon, and there goes my rest day. I need it, sir, and the horses need it. For myself, I can do more the rest of the week when I take one rest day than I ever could when I worked all seven days. The Lord knew what he was doing when he set aside the Sabbath."

"Well then," said Mr. Briggs, "I'll find another cab."

Polly came out of the house just as their visitor was leaving. "Who was that?"

"His name is Briggs," Jerry explained. "He's hired us several times. He came over to ask me to drive him to church. Said he would make it a regular thing."

"Did you tell him you would?"

"No, dear," Jerry answered. "If I did, there would go our Sundays. It would only be the beginning. Before long I'd be working all the time like I used to. I don't want to get into that rut again. I don't want to beat down the horses, either. I'm sorry if I disappointed you; I know we could use the money."

She put her arms around him. "You didn't disappoint me, Jerry. I love our Sundays as a family; just me and you and the kids. They need it; I need it; you say you need it. The horses probably need it, too."

Jerry looked at her, then grinned. "Well, even the Lord rested. I guess we shouldn't feel bad if we take a day off."

Briggs' feelings were strong enough that he stopped hiring our cab. When the other drivers heard about it, they gave Jerry a hard time over turning down a regular customer, especially when passengers were scarce and sometimes a cabby waited an hour or more before he picked up a fare.

It was about three weeks after this, as we came into the yard rather late, that Polly came across the road to meet us with the lantern.

"Jerry," she said excitedly, "do you remember that Mr. Briggs, the man who wanted you to drive him to church?" She stopped to catch her breath. "His wife sent her servant this afternoon to ask if you would take Mrs. Briggs out tomorrow."

"I thought they were using someone else."

"They were," Polly explained. "But the servant said that Mr. Briggs was not pleased with the other drivers. He says you're the best, and he wanted you to take his wife tomorrow."

"Well, I guess I could do that," Jerry answered. That night he hummed to himself as he cleaned my feet and coat and put things away.

After this, Briggs would hire Jerry's cab as before, though he never asked him again for Sunday. One Sunday Jerry did take me out, though, and I want to tell you how it happened.

Jerry was brushing my coat, when Polly came out of the house. "What is it?" Jerry asked her.

"Dinah Brown just came over and said her mother is sick and that she wants to go see her this afternoon. It's ten miles or more, she said, and out in the country. She wants you to take her and the baby, Jerry. She says she can't pay today, but she will as soon as she can."

Jerry said nothing for a moment, then, "There goes our afternoon. I'm tired, and the horses are tired."

"I know, dear," Polly agreed. "But surely it won't break a commandment if you take this woman to see her sick mother."

Jerry laughed. "You are a good preacher," he told her. "Yes, you are right. I'll take Jack;

he's the stronger. If we don't push too hard, it won't hurt him. Would you mind going over to Braydon's and telling him the situation and asking him if I could borrow his gig?" Braydon was the butcher, and he kept his shop closed on Sunday.

She was back before Jerry was finished with me, and said yes, Braydon was glad to lend us his vehicle. Then she went in the house and fixed Jerry a couple of sandwiches.

At ten o'clock we started. The butcher's light gig ran so easily that after the cab it was like pulling nothing.

As we headed out of London, I smelled the air and the grass, the country roads; oh, it was pleasant. I thought I was at Birtwick again.

Jerry let me set my own pace, and I hardly noticed the passing of time and distance, but we reached the farmhouse where we were going by early afternoon.

Their lane took us by an open field with a grove of trees on one side. Two cows grazed contentedly in the field.

The boy who met us showed Dinah inside, then asked us if we needed anything.

"If your cows won't mind," Jerry suggested, "there's nothing Jack would like better than to be put out into that field for an hour or two. He won't bother the cows, and it will be good for him."

"No problem," the young man responded. "And after you've done that, you can come inside and we'll fix you something to eat."

Jerry thanked him, but said he had brought his lunch and that he wanted to take a walk out in the meadow as he could never do this in London.

"Make yourself at home," the boy said, and we were left to ourselves.

Jerry even took my harness off. I didn't know whether to graze or roll in the grass or

lie down and sleep or take a run across the field. I was free to do what I wanted to do. It was wonderful.

Jerry looked as happy as I was. He sat down under a tree by the stream and read out of a little book he often carried with him.

We had been there about an hour, when he gave me a good feed of oats. Nearly another hour passed—all too quickly—and it was time to go.

We took our time coming home, and as it was Sunday, traffic was not so heavy, and the trip was easy.

CHAPTER 16

Poor Sam

N ot many cab horses were as well off as was I. For example, my driver was my owner, which made him want to treat me as well as he could. Besides, Jerry was a good man, and would have treated me well anyway.

A few owners had a large number of horses and cabs, and they rented them out to the drivers for a certain amount of money per day. The horses did not belong to the men who drove them, so all the driver cared about was getting as much out of the horse as possible. If a driver was thoughtless or cruel, the horse had it rough indeed.

Fortunately I didn't know this from experience, but I had heard it talked about on the cab stand. Governor, who ran our stand, loved horses, and if he saw one being treated particularly badly, he would speak up.

One day a shabby looking driver brought his horse in and the pitiful thing looked beat. The driver went by the nickname "Seedy Sam," and he looked it—dejected and miserable.

Governor greeted him: "The police will get after you for mistreating that horse, mister."

The driver threw a ragged blanket over the horse and turned to face Governor. "I'd like to go to the police! I'd like to put some people in jail! If someone is arrested for mistreating this horse, it ought not be me; it ought to be the man who charges me so much to rent him for the day; it ought to be the authorities who keep the fares so low."

Sam's feelings were hot, now, and he sounded almost desperate as he talked on.

"It takes eighteen shillings a day to pay for this cab and two horses. That means I've got to get nine shillings out of each horse before there's anything for me. I've seen fourteen, sixteen hours a day when I've not made more than that. Ask my wife. Ask my kids. They know."

Some of the other drivers had gathered around, and they nodded in agreement as Sam continued.

"I rent this cab from old Skinner, and he never gives a day off or a consideration. If I don't work hard, who does? I feel like an old man, and I'm not forty-five."

Sam held out his arms, showing where his jacket was worn and patched.

"Do you see this coat? Do I need a new one? Does this horse need a better blanket? I had to pawn my clock last week to pay Skinner."

I had never noticed before how thin Sam was, nor seen the wild, staring look in his eyes.

185

"I'm not of a kind to abuse a horse," Sam said, "but if it comes to it, a man has to put himself and his family before the horse. Yes, I'll admit it; I've used the whip, if that's what it takes."

Sam wasn't finished.

"Then last week I had a rider who accused me of cheating him. He said the fare was too much, and he counted it out like he was angry, grudging every penny. I wish he had to sit all day on a cab box, and squeeze out his living, bad weather and good, hot days and cold. It isn't right."

Sam was finished now, and the other drivers echoed his feelings.

Jerry had stayed out of this conversation, but I don't think I've ever seen his face so sad. Governor kept to one side, his hands in his pockets.

"I'm sorry I spoke of the police, Sam," Governor said. "I won't say more. Yes, these

are hard times. Hard times for a man; hard times for a horse."

Several days after this conversation, a new man came on the stand, with a cab that looked like Sam's.

"Isn't that Sam's cab?" one of the drivers asked.

"He's sick in bed," came the answer. "He took sick last night. He'd been out all day, and was pretty beat when he came in. The wife sent the boy to say he had a fever, so I'm using his cab."

The next morning we saw the same man, driving Sam's cab again.

"Is Sam any better?" Governor asked.

"He's no more."

"He's what?"

"He's dead."

"You don't mean Sam has died?"

"He died. Went fast, too," the man said. "Went out of his mind, raving about Skinner, then died."

Everyone was quiet. Finally, Governor broke the silence. "Let's take it as warning, lads. A warning for us."

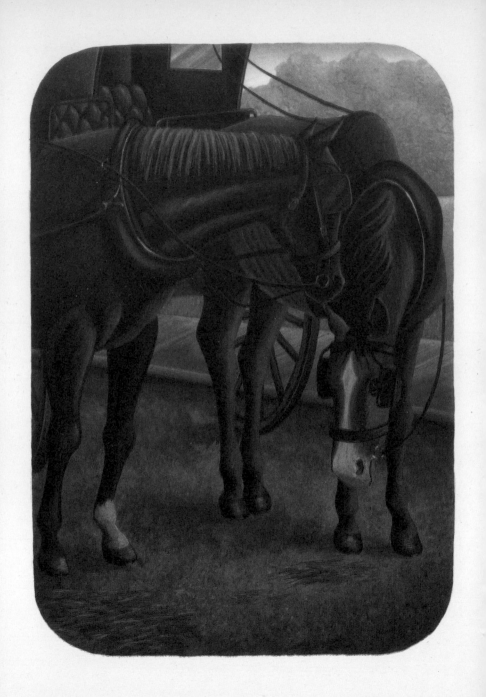

CHAPTER 17

I Meet Ginger Again

We were waiting outside one of the city parks where a band was playing when a run-down cab came and parked next to us. The horse was as shabby looking as the cab, a worn-out chestnut whose coat didn't look as if it had been brushed for days. The ribs showed through the skin, and the poor animal's knees were in bad shape.

I had been eating some of my hay, and the light breeze took a little of it over her way. It pained me to see how quickly that skinny neck came around and picked it up, and turned to me looking for more. Such a hopeless look in those dull eyes as they met mine.

Then I recognized her. Ginger! Before I could speak, she asked me, "Black Beauty, is that you?"

Yes, it was Ginger, but not the Ginger of old. Her graceful neck was thin and strained now. The joints in her poor legs were misshapen from heavy loads, and worst of all was the suffering which showed in her face.

I edged closer so we could have a talk, and what a story she had to tell.

I last saw her in the field at Earlshall, and after a little rest, she was sold. Things went well for awhile, but one day her owner drove her too hard, and the old problem with her back and lungs came back. Another trip to the horse doctor, a short rest, and she was sold again.

This happened more than once, and each time she sunk lower and lower.

"The master I have now," she told me, "owns a lot of cabs and horses and rents them by the day. You look as if you're doing well, and I'm glad. But how can I tell you what it's like for me?

"When this master found out my lungs were weak, he complained I wasn't worth keeping, and he put me with one of the worst drivers who'll work me till I drop.

"They say they're going to get their money out of me if they kill me, and they will. Maybe you can see the whip marks on my back. They don't care. Work, work, work. Never a rest. Work all week. On Sundays, too."

This wasn't the Ginger I knew. "I remember when you fought them if they mistreated you," I told her.

Her chest heaved and she gave out a long sigh. "Not any more. And what did it get me? I have to take it, now. I'll die. I hope I die at work and not be knocked in the head or shot."

I tried to think of something to comfort her, but just then her driver came. With a jerk at the reins, he backed her out and was gone, giving her a cut with the whip as he drove away.

CHAPTER 18

Election Day

When we saw our first fare, we should have known that Election Day would be busy for us.

We had been on the stand only a couple of minutes when a big fellow with a briefcase came up, in a hurry, of course.

"Bishopsgate Station," he snapped. Our next fare wanted to go to Regent's Park. Next we were called to a side street to take an older lady to the bank.

"Wait for me," she asked Jerry, her voice thin and trembling. "And you can take me back home."

I thought the next man was going to drive me himself! He ran up and almost dropped his sheaf of papers as he opened the door and plopped down. "Bow Street Police Station," he demanded. "Let's go!"

A couple more fares and we came back, and for a while were the only cab on the stand. Jerry knew we might go out at any minute, so he put on my nose-bag and gave me some oats.

Taking out his lunch, he said to me, "Better eat while we can, Jack."

Oh, the oats were good! Crushed oats, mixed with bran. After our busy morning, they tasted good! Can you see why I wanted to do my best for such a master?

The streets were full of people rushing here and there: cabs with various candidates' colors on them (Jerry wouldn't permit such a thing on our cab); workers taking voters to the polls. I saw two people knocked down by the traffic, and don't know if they were hurt or not.

I don't remember when we were so busy. It's good that elections don't come every day!

Jerry and I had eaten only a few bites when a young woman carrying a child came our way. She didn't seem to know where she was going. Seeing Jerry, she asked him how far it was to St. Thomas' Hospital. While she stood there, the child began to cry.

"Here," Jerry told her instantly, "get in. We'll take you. It's three miles, and you can't walk that far with that boy. He's too heavy for you to carry."

She looked bewildered. "Sir," she told Jerry, "I can't afford the ride."

"Get in," Jerry said again. "I said we'd take you. Please. Get in."

Just then two businessmen came up. "Hey! Cabbie!" they called. One of them already had the door open.

"Sirs," Jerry told them, "this cab is taken. She was here first."

"Oh, indeed?" came the response. They opened the door and got in. "She'll have to wait."

Jerry said nothing for a moment, then closed the door to the cab and turned his back upon the two men inside, saying as he did so, "Well, gentlemen, I hope you have a nice rest in there. We're not going anywhere."

A second later the door opened and the two men got out. They called Jerry all kinds of bad names, but he said nothing. "You'll hear about this," one of them said as they stomped off.

Now Jerry turned to the young mother. "Please. Get in. We'll take you and that little lad to the hospital."

It started to rain as we made our way through the traffic. At the hospital Jerry helped the young woman out of the cab and inside to the reception desk.

The rain was coming down hard now. Just as we were leaving the hospital we heard a woman's voice calling, "Cab!"

Jerry seemed to know the lady, though I had never seen her before. "Jeremiah Barker?" she asked him. "Is it you? I am glad to see you. With this being election day, I was afraid I would not find a cab in this part of London today."

"I'm glad to see you," Jerry said, then asked, "Where to, ma'am?"

"To Paddington Station," she told him.

We made it to the station in good time, and the woman stood a good while under the shelter talking to Jerry. I found out she had been Polly's mistress.

When she turned to go, she asked Jerry, "If you ever think of giving up cab work, please come and talk with me. Sometimes I know of a place that needs a good groom, and I would be glad to recommend you."

Then she pressed ten shillings into Jerry's hand. "Here's five shillings each for the two children; my gift for them."

Jerry watched until she was gone. Then we turned for home. I was tired, and Jerry probably was, too.

CHAPTER 19

Captain Has to Go

I had become good friends with Captain. It makes me sad even yet to think of how he came to leave us.

He had taken a rider to the railroad station when it happened. He and Jerry were coming back when they saw a brewery wagon heading toward them at a furious rate.

Brewer's wagons are heavy. They have to be strong to carry full barrels of whiskey. Brewer's horses are always of a big, strong breed, as well. Maybe you've seen them.

This wagon was empty, and the two horses were out of control and coming hard. The driver stood and pulled at the reins and yelled at the horses, but to no use. Worse, the street was full of traffic.

All of a sudden the dray knocked down a young girl and ran over her, then swerved and smashed into our cab. The impact tore the wheel off and turned our cab over, splintering the shafts. One of the shafts speared Captain in the side.

Jerry was knocked to the ground and bruised up a bit. But Captain was dragged several feet. His side was torn, and his shoulder was gashed, and he was cut in several places.

It was pitiful to see poor Captain come in that afternoon, the blood oozing from his side and shoulder, and limping from his wounds. I could tell he was badly hurt.

The wagon driver was drunk and had to pay a fine, and the brewer had to pay damages to our master. But who would pay for the damage to Captain?

The farrier did his best to ease Captain's pain. Jerry did his best for Captain, too. It took almost a week to repair our cab, so there were several days when I didn't go out. During that time, Jerry earned nothing.

Our first day back on the stand, Governor asked Jerry how Captain was.

"He'll never do cab work again," Jerry said, shaking his head. "The farrier told me this morning. He suggested I sell him as a cart horse."

Jerry's feelings showed as he continued. "Cart work! Cart work! I've seen what cart horses have to endure. I only wish that drunken drayman had to do cart work. Maybe if the drunks could break their own bones and smash their own wagons and cripple their own horses they might see the damage they cause."

Captain never returned to the stand. At first he seemed to do well, but it was only Jerry's care that saw him through. Captain was old, and he never regained his strength after the accident.

The farrier said he might get well enough to bring a few pounds at the sale, but Jerry said no, not for a few pounds would he condemn Captain to the life of a cart horse. Better, Jerry said, to put a bullet through Captain's heart than that. Hearing such talk didn't make me feel very good.

The next day or so Harry took me to the forge for some new shoes, and when we came back, Captain was gone. I felt the loss, and the family did, too.

Now Jerry needed a second horse. Someone told him about a young animal, a runaway who had smashed his owner's carriage and thrown his master to the pavement. The horse was scarred up a bit and no longer suitable for a rich man's stables, so the coachman was told to put him up for sale.

"He looks high spirited," Jerry told the seller. "But I don't mind that if he's not mean."

"No meanness in him, sir," the seller insisted. "His mouth is tender, and in my opinion his lordship caused the accident, though I wouldn't want to be quoted on that. He'd been penned up for a while, too, and when he was let out, he wanted to go."

Then, dropping his voice even lower, "And they had the curb on him; 'bearing rein,' they calls it. As tight as could be. No wonder the horse acted up."

So it was that Hotspur came to live with us. He was as tall as Captain, but brown instead, and only five years old. I gave him a greeting, but asked no questions.

Hotspur was restless that first night. He kept pulling at his halter rope, and banged against the side of his stall, keeping me awake.

I didn't know how this was going to work, but the second day Jerry took him out and worked him five or six hours in the cab. That burned off his energy, and Hotspur and I both slept that night.

I came to like him. It was a comedown to him that he was a cab horse, after living on a gentleman's farm. He didn't like to wait at the cab stand, either. He'd rather be moving.

But after a week he told me that being rid of the bearing rein made up for a great deal. He said cab work was not so bad after all.

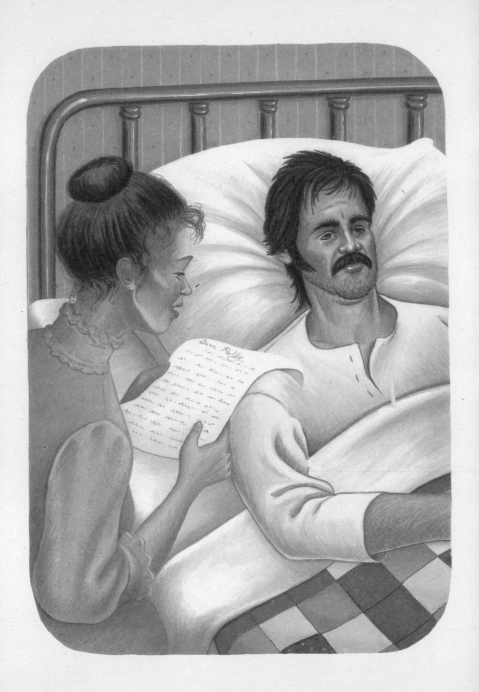

CHAPTER 20

Jerry Makes a Change

Maybe you like Christmas and New Year's, but for cabbies and their horses, it's no holiday. With all the parties, it's our busiest time.

Though it's good to work, and good to be paid, it can be a difficult time for us. It's no fun to wait for hours, shivering in the cold, while people inside are warm and laughing.

Do the men and women enjoying their party give a thought to the cabbie, or the cabbie's horse, freezing outside?

Jerry was afraid of Hotspur's lungs, so I was usually the one who worked the afternoons and evenings. Christmas Week we had a great deal of late calls, and Jerry took a bad cough.

No matter how late we came home, Polly always waited up. Several times I thought her face looked worried.

New Year's Eve we had to take two gentlemen to a house in the West End. We delivered them at nine, and they told us to come back at eleven, which we did. Jerry was always prompt.

While we waited, the clock chimed the quarter hours, and then struck twelve. But the door stayed shut and the party inside kept going. Through the window we could see they were playing cards. This might take awhile.

During the day it had rained, but the wind changed and now it started sleeting; hard, driving sheets of bitter icy sleet. Jerry got off his box and came around and pulled one of my cloths up over me, but I was still cold.

He was, too. He stamped his feet and beat his arms, but that set him off coughing, so he opened the door and sat on the cab floor with his feet on the ground. At least he was out of the wind. But there was no protection from the cold.

At half-past twelve, Jerry went to the front door and rang the bell. When the servant came, Jerry asked if he would be needed that night.

"Yes, indeed. Don't leave; it's almost over."

So Jerry sat down again. His coughing was harder.

Finally, after one o'clock, the door to the house opened and the men got into the cab and told Jerry where to drive. We went nearly two miles.

My legs were so stiff from the cold that I was afraid I might slip, as the roads were icy. Neither man said one word about making us wait. In fact, they grumbled about the fare, and told Jerry they didn't think they should have to pay for the time he waited. It was hard earned money.

By the time we made it home, Jerry was so hoarse he could hardly talk, and his cough was worse than ever.

"Can I help?" Polly asked.

"Yes," he whispered. "Get Jack something you've warmed a bit, and then fix something hot for me."

Tired and sick as he was, Jerry still gave me a rubdown, and climbed into the hayloft for

extra straw. Polly gave me the warm mash, and they left.

The next day no one came till mid morning, and then it was Harry. He fed me and Hotspur, and cleaned out the stalls, and then put more straw in, as if it were Sunday. That's how I knew we were not going out.

Usually Harry talked to us, but not today. At noon he came back, his mother with him, and she was crying. From the way they talked, I knew Jerry was sick and that the Doctor had come and it was bad.

Two more days passed and still we didn't go out. Harry came, or Dolly. Not Jerry. We didn't see their mother, either; she stayed with Jerry.

Another day came, and Harry was cleaning the stable when there was a tap at the door. It was Governor, from the cab stand.

"I wondered how your father is, my boy," he said.

Harry stopped for a moment. "He's not so good," he said. "The doctor says it is 'bronchitis,' and it can't be much worse. The doctor says his fever's really high."

Governor shook his head. "I knew he was sick when he didn't come to work. I'm sorry, son, that your father's sick. Looks like you've got everything done here. I'll stop in tomorrow morning."

The next morning Governor came again, and this time Harry said his father was better.

"Good; good," said Governor. Then he turned to us. "Say, Harry; let me give you a suggestion about the horses. It won't hurt Jack to have a good rest; he could use it. You might take him for a turn or two down the street and back. But Hotspur needs to work, or when you take him out he'll be so unruly no one can manage him."

"He's that way now," said Harry. "I've kept him on short rations, but he's so lively I don't think I could drive him."

Governor rubbed his chin. "I think I can help with that. Ask your mother if she'll let me come and take him out and work him. I'll do it every day till Jerry gets better. Whatever he earns, I'll give your mother half."

And so Governor came and took Hotspur out. Polly tried again and again to thank him, but every time she started to say something, Governor brushed it aside, saying his horses needed a rest anyway.

Jerry kept improving, but the doctor said no more cab work for him. More than once I heard the children talking to each other, wondering how they could earn money to help the family.

One afternoon while Harry was grooming Hotspur, Dolly came in, excited.

"Do you know who lives at Fairstowe?" she asked her brother. "A letter came for mother from Fairstowe, and she is showing it to father."

217

"Fairstowe," Harry repeated. "That's the place where mother's old mistress lives. You know, the lady who sent you and me the money last summer."

"Wonder what she is writing to mother about."

"Mother wrote to her," said Harry. "She told dad if he ever wanted to give up cab work, to let her know. So mother did."

Dolly went back inside, leaving Harry scrubbing away at Hotspur. Minutes later she was back.

"Harry! Harry!" she told him, jumping up and down. "Mrs. Fowler wants us to come live near them. There's an empty cottage, and it has a hen house and a garden. She wants father to be her coachman."

That was good news for the family, but bad news for me. Good-bye to the best master I'd ever had. Good-bye to the children.

Besides, the years had taken their toll. As old as I was, who would want me now?

CHAPTER 21

A Hard Master

My new master was Nicholas Skinner, and he was as cruel as his name. His face was mean and harsh. The very sound of his voice was unpleasant. If I'm not mistaken, he was the man who drove Seedy Sam to his death.

Skinner's operation was thoroughly bad. I thought I had worked hard before; I was wrong. I never knew till now what utter misery felt like.

Skinner was hard on his drivers and the drivers took it out on us horses.

It was the heat of summer, and we worked seven days a week. A Sunday rest? Not in this place. Several times I was hired out on a Sunday morning by four or five men celebrating their day off, and had to take them ten or fifteen miles out in the country and back again.

Five men, plus the cab driver. Do you think those men ever thought of getting out when we came to a hill and lightening my load? Never. Many times after such a trip I came home so feverish and hot that I could not eat.

If only I could be back with Jerry. If only someone would say a kind word. If only I could have one of Jerry's treats—a bran mash to cool me down, or a carrot—and have Saturday night and Sunday off. If only I could go to work on Monday morning rested for once.

My driver cared nothing for his horse. He had a whip with metal in it which could draw blood, and he used it often. He would even whip me under the belly and around my head.

My best was not enough for him. His cruelty took the heart out of me.

I remembered what Ginger had told me. Now I was in the same situation.

One morning, having come to the stand at eight o'clock, I had done a good share of work when we had to take a fare to the train.

After our fare left us, my driver pulled up at the end of a line of waiting cabs. The train was coming in, and he hoped he could get a fare for the return trip.

This was a long train. One by one the cabs were taken, and our turn came. We were called by a family: man, wife, two children, and lots of luggage. The woman and little boy got into the cab and the man directed the porter who was piling the baggage onto the luggage rack. The little girl came around and looked at me.

"Father," she told her dad, "this horse can't take us and all the suitcases. It's too much."

The driver spoke up. "Don't worry about him, missy. He's strong."

The porter handling the heavy bags suggested that perhaps the gentleman wanted to take a second cab for part of the load.

This upset the girl's father, and he turned to my driver. "What do you say? Can your horse do it or not?"

"Oh, certainly. Nothing to worry about." Then, to the porter, "Send up the boxes. He can take that load and more."

One of the boxes was so heavy I could hear the springs creak under the weight.

The little girl was almost crying. "Please, papa. Put them in another cab. It's too much."

"Hush up," said her father. "Don't make such a fuss. The driver knows if the horse can do it or not. Get in and stop that."

The driver slapped the reins across my back and I dragged the load out of the station.

I had not rested nor eaten since early morning, but I did my best. Things were bear-

able until we came to Ludgate Hill. I was try-ing to keep up—I wouldn't have needed the whip but he gave me slash after slash—when, quicker than I can tell you about it, my feet slipped and I fell on my side. The force of it knocked the breath out of me.

I couldn't move. I thought I was going to die; and felt like it. I heard the bustle of peo-ple and voices, and could hear men unloading the cab, but it was all like a dream.

"He's dead," someone said.

I heard a policeman ordering people away, but I could not open my eyes. It was all I could do to gasp for air.

Someone threw cold water on my head, and I remember a blanket being thrown over me.

Gradually my senses came back. I could feel someone patting me and encouraging me to stand up. I tried, but couldn't make it, and tried again. Finally, I managed to get to my feet.

Someone led me to a close by stable and put me in a stall and brought a warm gruel, which I drank.

By evening I was strong enough to go back to Skinner's. They probably did as much as they knew to do, but I was almost sorry to see the place again.

The next morning the farrier came and examined me.

"He's not diseased," the farrier said. "He's overworked. He needs a rest. Several months. You can't work him now; he'll not be able to stand it."

"Then he's finished with me," said Skinner. "I'm not running a hospital for sick horses. If he can't work, then it's the end for him."

I shivered, hearing such talk, but the farrier offered a suggestion. "He's not broken-winded," he told Skinner. "If he were, he ought to be killed, but he's not. There's a sale coming up in a couple of weeks. Why not rest him and feed him and see if he perks up,

and you might get something out of him at the sale."

Skinner wasn't too excited about feeding me and letting me off work, but when he thought he might get a little more than whatever my skin would bring, he decided to see what rest and food would do.

Twelve days later they took me to the sale. Anyplace would be better than this. I resolved to hold up my head and hope for the best.

CHAPTER 22

Willie Takes
a Chance

T he sale was a dreary experience. I was
put with the lowest kind of horses;
horses that were broken down, lame,
broken winded, old, and sick. Some of them
were so bad it would have been merciful to
shoot them.

The sellers and the buyers were not a high
class lot, either. Many of them looked as bad
as the horses. There were men who were old
and poor and who were trying to get a horse
to pull their little woodcart or to haul coal.
There were men who, rather than have the
horse sold for its skin and knocked in the

231

head, were trying to get two or three pounds for it instead.

There were all kinds of characters. Some men may have been poor, but they had a voice and manner I knew I could trust. Others were harsh and cutting in their speech, and I knew they would be the same with a whip.

There was an older man, a farmer, who took a liking to me. He had been up in the area where the better horses were for sale, and came down where we were to look things over. Right away I knew I could work for him. Oh, if he would only buy me!

He had a boy with him, his grandson, probably. The two of them stood for a moment and measured me with their eyes. My mane still looked good, and my tail. I turned to look at him and tried to stand straight.

"Willie," said the man, "there's a horse which has known better days."

"Grandpa," the boy said. "Do you think he was ever a carriage horse?"

"I would say so, my boy," the man said, moving nearer. "When he was young, he could have been a fine horse. A gentleman's horse, maybe. Look at the ears and the nostrils. See his shoulder and neck? There's good blood in that horse."

He reached over to pat me, and I put my face over to him. The boy came and rubbed my nose.

"Grandpa," the boy suggested, "he likes us. Could you buy him and make him young again like you did Ladybird?"

"Lad, I can't make all horses young. Besides, Ladybird was not old. She was mistreated."

"Grandpa, this one's not old," the boy insisted. "Look at him. He's thin, but his eyes are good. Look in his mouth, Grandpa. He's not old."

The man who was selling me chimed in now. "The lad has a point, sir. This horse was used hard in the cabs. That's why he's run down. What he needs is a six month layoff.

You could give five for him and by next spring he'd be worth twenty."

"See, Grandpa," said the boy. "See?"

The farmer felt my legs, which were strained and swollen from my ordeals in the cab. He looked into my mouth. "I'd say he is thirteen or fourteen. Could you bring him out for me?"

I arched my neck and raised my tail a little while the seller put me through my paces. My legs were stiff, but I did the best I could.

"What is the least you will take?" asked the farmer as he looked at me again.

The seller cleared his throat, and then told the man the price. "My master said don't take less than five, sir. Five pounds."

"Well," the farmer said, drawing his money out of his pocket, "I'm taking a chance, I know."

The seller counted the money, then offered, "I can take him to the inn for you, sir."

"Thank you," said the old man. "That would be fine."

I followed as they led me. The boy was as happy as if it were Christmas. The grandfather seemed pleased as well. At the inn, I had a good feed, then was ridden home by one of my new master's farmhands.

When I reached my new place I was turned into a fenced-in field with a shed in one corner for shelter. Imagine my joy at such wonderful surroundings.

The man and his grandson came to look at me. "Willie," said the grandfather, "you're in charge of him. See that he gets oats and hay every morning and evening, and give him the run of the field during the day."

The boy undertook his new job with enthusiasm. He paid me a visit every day, sometimes bringing me a carrot or some other treat. What a difference from Skinner's place. How I pitied those poor horses still there.

Willie gave me pats and kind words and called me "Old Crony." He even came into the field and I would follow him around. When he brought me in for the night he was really careful, and checked my coat and my feet to be sure I was all right.

The old man came, too, and checked to see how I was doing. "You're succeeding, Willie," he said. He's getting better. We'll see a difference come spring."

It's amazing what good food and enough rest and proper exercise can do. I could feel the change myself. The good care I had when I was young, and my good health from my mother showed now, and I could feel myself growing stronger as the days went by.

One day in early spring Willie's grandfather said he would try me in the carriage. It was nice to be out, and he and Willie both drove me. We didn't go very far, but it was easy work for me. The old stiffness was gone, and I was not even tired when we came in.

After that the two of them took me out for short trips, so I would become used to working again. How good it was to feel strong once more!

"Aren't you glad you bought him?" the boy asked.

"Yes," his grandfather agreed.

"Grandpa," Willie told the old man, "now we have to find him a good home."

CHAPTER 23

Home at Last

Oʜne summer day as the groom was cleaning me, I noticed that he did it with more care than usual. He took shears and trimmed my fetlocks and legs. He used the tarbrush on my hoofs. He polished the harness. He even parted the lock of hair on my forehead. Something was up.

I could tell from the way he worked on me that a change was coming. I could have told it from Willie, too. He was excited, and sad, nervous and glad, all at the same time.

Even his grandfather acted a little differently.

No one had said anything in my hearing, so I was not sure, but in my mind I thought perhaps we were going to a sale. And of course, who were they selling but me?

But we didn't go to a sale at all. I was hitched to the carriage and we began to drive down the road.

"If the ladies like him," grandfather said, "they'll get a good horse. It'll be good for Old Crony, too."

Now I knew.

We continued for a while, my wondering all the time what was going to happen, when the old man stopped at a nice little house with a proper lawn and shrubs in the yard. There was even a driveway.

Willie hopped out and rang the bell.

"Is Miss Blomefield or Miss Ellen at home?"

They were indeed.

Willie came back to the carriage and stayed with me. His grandfather went inside. I thought he was not coming back, but it was probably only ten minutes or so.

He came out followed by three ladies, one of them tall and sort of pale, being helped by a much younger woman who had a smile when she saw me.

The third woman was dignified and graceful. She was Miss Blomefield.

All three were looking at me, and started asking one question after another.

The younger one, she was Miss Ellen, said she thought she liked me.

"He has a good face," were her words. I liked her manner and the way she smiled. Then she saw my knees "What's wrong with his knees?"

Miss Blomefield spoke up. "He's fallen."

Lavina, the tall one, threw up her hands. "Oh, dear! I once saw a horse fall, and it's frightful. Frightful! We can't have a horse that's not steady. What if he goes down again?"

If only I could tell her how those scars came. I began to be nervous myself. Can't

someone say something? Willie's grandfather stepped in.

"You see, ladies," he said evenly, "many a good horse has had a poor driver. I've seen animals hurt by accident, or through carelessness. It isn't always the fault of the horse. This one, now, is as sure and steady as you can find."

Miss Ellen looked at him, and looked again at me. But he wasn't finished.

"In fact, if you want to take him and try him for a while, I'll agree, and after you've had him awhile, your coachman can let me know if you want to keep him." He looked at the boy. "What do you say, lad? Are you agreeable?"

Willie stood up straighter and tried to make his voice sound deep. "Yes. I agree."

Miss Blomefield almost smiled at that, then offered her opinion. "You've always helped us with your advice, and your recommendation is enough for me. If my sister sees no objection, then we will accept your offer of a trial period." She looked at Willie. "And thank you, son, for the offer."

Willie nodded, but kept quiet.

Next morning Willie and his grandfather came early. The old man brushed my coat and made sure my feet looked nice, and Willie combed out my tail and my mane.

They had barely finished when a young man came to the stable to take me away.

He seemed pleased enough with me until he noticed my knees. "I did not think you would recommend to my ladies a horse with knees like that."

"You're only taking him on approval," said Grandfather. "I think you'll be pleased. If he's not what you want, we'll be glad to have him back." He looked at Willie, who nodded his head. Willie wasn't going to say anything. It looked to me like there were tears in his eyes.

So I was led away again, to a comfortable stable where they fed me and left me alone the rest of the day. The next morning the groom came and gave me a going over. As he was cleaning my face, and especially the white marking, he started talking to himself.

"This looks like the star Black Beauty had. It's the same." He stands about the same height, too. I wonder...."

He stepped back and looked me over carefully, still talking under his breath.

"White star on his forehead. White forefoot, too." He felt in my coat in the middle of my back. "Well I never! Here's the patch of white John called 'Beauty's three-penny bit.' This is Beauty! It's Black Beauty!" Then he patted my face and spoke to me: "Do you remember me, Beauty? I'm Joe Green, who almost killed you when I was little."

I didn't remember, because he was a man, now. But he knew me. I moved closer to show we were friends. Joe Green. After all this time, he remembered me.

"They have you here on trial," Joe said. "We'll give you a try, old fellow. I wish John

Manly were here. He would be so glad. What happened to those knees, Beauty? You've had some hard days, I'll wager. But you won't have them here. I'll see to that."

That afternoon Joe hitched me to a light carriage and drove me around to the front of the house. Miss Ellen wanted to try me out, and Joe went with her. She was a good driver, and seemed pleased with my work.

Joe told her about me, and how he was sure I was Squire Gordon's Black Beauty, and how I had saved the mistress' life.

When we came back, the other sisters came around to hear how I did, and she told them what Joe had told her about me.

Miss Ellen said she was going to write a letter to Mrs. Gordon and tell her that her favorite horse had come to their place.

Someone took me out every day for the next week, and when everyone was convinced I was safe, Miss Lavina finally dared to try me.

That was the end of the testing. All three sisters decided they wanted to keep me, and to give me my old name, "Black Beauty."

I have lived here for a whole year. Joe is the best groom, and takes such good care. My work is agreeable, and I feel my strength coming back. My spirits have lifted, too; the old gloom has vanished.

Willie and his grandfather came by the other day and asked about me. Joe brought them around, and I heard Grandfather tell the boy, "With the care he's getting here, he'll live till he's twenty. Maybe even longer."

Willie comes when he can. The sisters promised him that I'll never be sold, so that fear is gone. I'm at home now. Sometimes in the mornings when I'm still half asleep, it seems like I'm back at Birtwick again, standing under the apple trees, with my old friends.